WINNIPEG
WITHDRAWN
LIBRARY

D0066237

JAN 1 0 2020

LEAP *of* FAITH

LEAP *of* FAITH

KIMBERLY BRUBAKER BRADLEY

Dial Books for Young Readers

DIAL BOOKS FOR YOUNG READERS
A division of Penguin Young Readers Group • Published by The Penguin Group
Penguin Group (USA) Inc., 375 Hudson Street, New York, NY 10014, U.S.A.

Penguin Group (Canada), 90 Eglinton Avenue East, Suite 700, Toronto, Ontario, Canada
M4P 2Y3 (a division of Pearson Penguin Canada Inc.) • Penguin Books Ltd, 80 Strand,
London WC2R 0RL, England • Penguin Ireland, 25 St. Stephen's Green, Dublin 2, Ireland
(a division of Penguin Books Ltd) • Penguin Group (Australia), 250 Camberwell Road,
Camberwell, Victoria 3124, Australia (a division of Pearson Australia Group Pty Ltd) •
Penguin Books India Pvt Ltd, 11 Community Centre, Panchsheel Park, New Delhi - 110
017, India • Penguin Group (NZ), Cnr Airborne and Rosedale Roads, Albany, Auckland
1310, New Zealand (a division of Pearson New Zealand Ltd) • Penguin Books (South
Africa) (Pty) Ltd, 24 Sturdee Avenue, Rosebank, Johannesburg 2196, South Africa •
Penguin Books Ltd, Registered Offices: 80 Strand, London WC2R 0RL, England

Copyright © 2007 by Kimberly Brubaker Bradley
All rights reserved

The publisher does not have any control over and does not assume any
responsibility for author or third-party websites or their content.

Designed by Nancy R. Leo-Kelly
Text set in Bembo • Printed in the U.S.A.
1 3 5 7 9 10 8 6 4 2

Library of Congress Cataloging-in-Publication Data
Bradley, Kimberly Brubaker.
Leap of faith / Kimberly Brubaker Bradley.
p. cm.
Summary: Forced to attend a Catholic middle school because of her conduct,
Abigail discovers a talent for theater and develops a true religious faith.
ISBN-13: 978-0-8037-3127-1
[1. Catholic schools—Fiction. 2. Schools—Fiction. 3. Behavior—Fiction.]
I. Title.
PZ7.B7247Lea 2007 [Fic]—dc22 2006021322

To Bart Bradley and Christopher Robinette,
with thanks to Rev. Timothy E. Keeney
for the unofficial imprimatur

LEAP of FAITH

Prologue

We sat in the front row of the church. The lights, which had been dimmed all along, went out entirely. The people in the pews murmured softly, and many of them, including Mrs. Brashares, leaned back and looked over their shoulders toward the door. I was caught by the light pouring in through one of the prismed side windows, bathing the lilies on the altar in a silver glow. "Look at the moonlight," I whispered.

"That's not moonlight, it's from the light in the parking lot," Mrs. Brashares whispered back.

I was trying to be spiritual; you'd think she would indulge me.

Nothing seemed to be happening. The church had gone still, silent, waiting. Every pew was full, including the one toward the back and off to one side where my parents sat. I wondered if the people surrounding them were saying rosaries or mumbling in Latin or doing something else to set them on edge. I no longer wanted them to be uncomfortable in church, which I knew was progress. On the other hand, I didn't especially care if they were comfortable tonight. Tonight was mine.

Still nothing happened. Seconds, then minutes, ticked by. "When does it start?" I whispered.

"Soon," murmured Mrs. Brashares.

"What do I do with this little candle?" I asked. It was halfway between a birthday candle and the sort you'd stick on your dining room table. One of the ushers gave it to me when I walked in. Everyone had one.

"You'll see," said Mrs. Brashares. "Shh."

"It's super-cool," Chris added over my shoulder. I looked. He wasn't supposed to be here, up front in the reserved seats. They were only for the special people, like his mom and me. "Stinks sitting by myself," he said. "Scoot over. Pretend I'm your godparent."

"I'm too old for a godparent."

"Pretend you're younger."

"Shh!" his mom said. She didn't make him move back, and I was glad. Mrs. Brashares was my sponsor, but Chris was my partner in crime.

Something moved in the darkness at the back of the church. "Here we go," Chris said.

I took a quick deep breath. My heart beat fast. I looked up at the crucifix, hidden in the shadow thrown by the parking lot lights. What would Jesus do here? I figured, if lightning was going to strike, it would happen now.

CHAPTER
1

School had been in session for two weeks on the Tuesday morning my parents shoved me through the principal's door at St. Catherine's. I had to be shoved; my feet stubbed against the carpet. I didn't want another principal's office. I didn't want another principal. I slumped in the chair where they put me and I stared at my hands.

"Don't slouch," my mother said.

I slouched harder.

"Abigail," she whispered.

"What?" I whispered back furiously. Since last week—since what my parents liked to call "the accident," as though what had happened had not been my deliberate action—anger kept shooting out of me at unexpected times. I didn't know who I was most angry at. Top choices included Brett McAvery, both my parents, and middle school principals of any sort.

And myself. Maybe I was first on my list. Who knew? Not me, that was sure.

I'd been straight-out expelled from public middle school at the very beginning of sixth grade. It was a record, the superintendent of schools told my parents. No other student had ever been kicked out as fast as me.

And no, I couldn't go back. Not ever. The weapons policy was very strict. I could go to the county alternative school with the drug-abusing high-schoolers and pregnant fourteen-year-olds, or I could be homeschooled and the county would send a tutor to my house once a week.

Or I could go to a private school, if my parents could find one that would take me. Hence this meeting with the principal of St. Catherine's.

From the silence in the room I realized everyone was looking at me. I saw a tiny piece of dirt under one of my fingernails, and slid my thumbnail across it to push it out.

My mother sighed. "She's not usually like this," she said, presumably to the principal. "She's very quiet—she's never gotten so much as detention before. Never gets in trouble—"

My father cleared his throat. "Abigail's always been a good girl. Before this. She . . . well—" He stopped. My parents had heard the story from so many sides—mine and Brett McAvery's and the middle school's and the teacher who was on lunchroom duty—that they weren't sure who was telling the truth and who was lying. Sometimes they wanted to believe me, but of course they didn't. It made them culpable if they did. They didn't want any of this mess to be my fault, but they absolutely especially also didn't want it to be theirs.

We preferred no-fault expulsions in my family.

We preferred silence. We preferred to put up with things.

We didn't complain. We did not get angry. Except of course for me. Made me wonder, sometimes, what I was even doing in my family.

Q

Flash backward a week, to the last time I sat in a principal's office. My mother burst through the door, dressed in her expensive suit and heels. She stopped dead when she saw me, and her mouth dropped open. She stared at my arm, at the streaks of blood running down it. They'd taken my knife away first thing, the teachers who had tackled me.

My mother stood gasping, like she had personally run all the way from her downtown office. She looked up at the principal, Mr. McAvery—who was plenty angry, let me tell you, given that it was his kid I'd just sent to the emergency room—and said, "It's true?"

Mr. McAvery's face was reddish purple. He'd been pacing up and down in front of me, not saying a word, but his face growing more and more purple all the time. "You bet it's true!" he roared, and went on from there, his words billowing out like steam escaping a pressure cooker.

I stared at my tennis shoes. One had a funny red splotch on it, and I reached down to touch it before I realized it was blood. Brett McAvery's, not mine. Same as on my arms.

The office door burst open again. This time it was a policeman. My mother let out another little gasp. Then my father came in, also at a run. "Is she hurt?" he asked my mother. My mother shook her head. "Is it true?" he asked.

In all this time Mr. McAvery hadn't stopped yelling. He was telling me off to the policeman now. "It's true," my mother said quietly.

I expected one of them to touch me, but neither did, as though what I'd done was contagious.

♧

"So?" the court-ordered shrink said, a few days later. "They really weren't angry? Not at all?"

I shrugged. I hated the shrink on sight. She wore too much jewelry and her hair was an unnatural color. Also, I didn't like her shoes. "Angry maybe that they had to miss work," I said. "That's all."

It was the truth too. You'd think they'd be angry, but my parents weren't. They talked in low voices to each other and seemed to be avoiding me.

The shrink was supposed to make sure I wasn't psychotic or something. She gave me a test that was so obvious, I answered wrong on purpose. She would say a word, and I was supposed to say the first word that came to my mind. "School," she said, and I answered, "Satan." For every word she said I answered *death,* or *hate,* or *kill.*

At the end of it she looked at me and said, "So, you're not angry?"

"Not really," I said. "No." The shrink seemed completely untrustworthy. Court-ordered? Like she was going to be on my side.

I was angry at the *shrink.* At the end she said, "That's all I need in order to make my recommendation, Abby. But I think maybe it'd be nice if you came to see me again. Maybe your parents could come too."

Ha. Fat chance.

Fast forward a week, and here I sat at St. Catherine's, and still no one was angry.

Except maybe me. My hands shook.

The St. Catherine's principal, a short man I barely glanced at as we walked in, cleared his throat. In a quiet voice he said that he'd telephoned Mr. McAvery after talking to my parents yesterday.

I wanted to run right out the door. I would never be safe here now that this guy was on Mr. McAvery's side. Mr. McAvery would never forgive me for what I'd done.

The principal cleared his throat again. A bad sign. "I don't think we'd have any trouble accepting Abigail as a student," he said. "We have an anti-bullying rule, and a strict code of conduct."

"Please don't be concerned," my mother said. "We'll make sure Abigail will behave from now on. She's never—"

The principal cut her off. "I meant that the other way. I

don't think she'll need to *defend* herself from anyone here."

I jerked my head up, and by chance looked the principal right in the eye. Had I heard that right? He looked straight back at me, calm and unsmiling. *Defend myself?* Wow. I looked back at my lap, and heard myself exhale. I waited for my parents to hear what he'd said—that maybe, just maybe, I wasn't the only person to blame.

"Fine," my father said, a little too heartily. "That's fine, then. When can she start? Tomorrow?"

"Tomorrow," agreed the principal. "And you should know that children quite often begin at St. Catherine's after the normal start of the year. There'll be no need to mention your reasons for sending Abigail here, unless you wish to."

Even looking at my lap I could feel the tension ooze out of my parents. How wonderful; how understanding; how fair.

There'd been something like two hundred witnesses to the fact that I'd attacked Brett McAvery in the school cafeteria, but by chance there'd also been a bus accident in our town the exact same day. The headlines got taken up by the drunken bus driver, not by me. So I wasn't notorious.

One second ago I had been grateful for that, would have begged this man not to share my record with my new teachers. But now I felt another flash of anger. Was I so bad we had to hide the truth?

My parents began discussing class size and the curriculum for the sixth grade, as though those things somehow mattered. "And of course, religion," the principal said. "As a Catholic school, we require daily religion classes for all our students, no matter what their faith background."

"We don't actually go to church," my father said.

I raised my head. "We don't actually believe in God."

"Abigail!" my mother said. "Of course we do!"

"Not me," I said.

My mother couldn't decide whether she should act angry or sad. She settled on a mixture of both, her eyebrows arched, her lips pursed. My father looked as if he'd like to slap me into yesterday.

Of course, violence was not condoned at this school. We had an anti-bullying rule and a strict code of conduct.

I looked hard at the principal for the first time. He was bald and plump, with round glasses that made his face and stomach look even rounder. He wore a black shirt with a funny white collar and a black sport coat. I looked at all that black, and I realized I'd just said I didn't believe in God to a Catholic priest.

"I'm sorry," I said.

"Don't be," he said. "I think honesty is the first step in any road to faith."

That made my father nervous. "See here," he said quickly, "we don't want her converted. I mean, our faith—our religion—it's fine with us. We don't want anybody messing with Abigail's mind."

The priest/principal turned his pale eyes toward my father. "Over half our student body is non-Catholic," he said. "We do not attempt to evangelize anybody." He looked at me. "You'll have to learn what you're taught in religion class," he said. "You won't have to believe it."

I nodded. "Good."

My parents switched the topic to uniforms, and school supplies, and which math class I'd be in. Then the priest asked me, "And which elective?"

I'd been picking my fingernails again. "Hmm?" I asked.

"Sixth grade is middle school; middle-schoolers get an elective. Do you want art, computers, economics, journalism—"

"Art," I said.

"No," my father said. "She wants something academic."

I thought of the freedom of a white sheet of paper, a good dark pen. "I want art."

"I'm not paying this kind of tuition for you to take art," my father said. "Pick something else."

Not like he'd wanted to send me here; not like I'd given him a choice. I knew the tuition was expensive. We wouldn't be going to the beach this summer, my mother had said.

"I love art," I whispered.

"Honey," my mother said, "pick something else. Any other thing you want."

I looked at the principal. "Computers," he repeated, "economics, journalism, Spanish, drama—"

"Drama." The only class more useless than art.

"Abigail!" my father said.

"You don't want to take drama," said my mother. "How about economics? That sounds fun. Think about it, honey. You've never been very dramatic."

Except for that one moment, when I had a knife in my hand.

"Drama," I said, and did not give in.

CHAPTER

2

The next day, Mrs. Moffett, my new homeroom teacher at St. Catherine's, assigned me to the care of a chunky, flat-faced girl named Jenna. "You've got the same schedule," the teacher told Jenna. "Please show her around."

Jenna nodded. "Okay," she said. Jenna was neutral, neither friendly nor mean. She wasn't the type to waste time with questions.

Which was just about perfect as far as I was concerned. The night before I'd endured an hour-long lecture about starting over and giving myself a new chance. The subtext was: *You'd better not screw up this time.* I'd decided the safest thing was to become invisible. It wasn't hard. I tucked myself behind Jenna's bulk as she moved through the hallways, and I felt like I was wearing the invisibility cloak from the Harry Potter books, strong and light. No one saw me at all.

First period after homeroom was math. "We're in the high class," Jenna said. "The smart kids." There were only eight students. St. Catherine's must have had a lot of stupid kids.

Second period was English, and it looked like all the same students as homeroom. When I said so, Jenna shrugged.

"Duh," she said, not unkindly. "They don't split English. This is the whole sixth grade. Twenty-two of us."

"That's all?" Dunbarton Middle School had two hundred per grade.

Jenna shrugged again. "It's pretty big for this school. Half of us have been here since kindergarten."

I'd gone to Reed Creek Elementary from kindergarten through fifth. Up until fourth grade I'd liked school. Fifth grade Brett McAvery changed everything.

Third period was science; fourth period was lunch. Pizza slices, three per person served cold out of a delivery box, and a few limp baby carrots and a cookie. I stared at my tray. Lunchrooms were always difficult, with all the unwritten rules about who could sit where. Maybe Jenna's friends wouldn't like me sitting at her table. Or maybe Jenna was wildly unpopular, and the moment I sat down beside her, I'd catch her unpopularity like the flu.

Did I mind? Was unpopular different from invisible?

In fifth grade I'd hung out at the edge of the popular crowd. During my two weeks at Dunbarton the rules had been different; I still sat at the edge of the in crowd, but I didn't belong there anymore.

Brett McAvery was the in-crowd. Brett McAvery was cute, and funny, and smart, and no one wanted to believe that he tormented me. My former best friend, Stacy, had been convinced I was lying.

"Brett would *never* do that!" she said, with a toss of her

15

perfect hair. "You're just making stuff up, Abigail. Are you that desperate for attention? It's pathetic."

And when I tried to complain to the principal—before I realized that Brett was his son—Brett came in with a choirboy face and told his dad he didn't understand why I was lying about him.

I blinked. I was still standing in the cafeteria of St. Catherine's. I had to stop thinking about Brett. That's what my mom said. Pretend it didn't happen.

Jenna nudged my side. "We go back to homeroom," she said. "We eat in our classrooms on Mass days."

"What days?"

"Wednesdays. Mass days. We go to church on Wednesdays."

I hadn't heard about that. "What do the non-Catholics do?"

She frowned. "Go to church. What do you think?"

"Why?"

She sounded exasperated. "Because you do."

As I walked into the classroom I tripped on the edge of the rug. I hadn't been looking down, and I didn't know the rug was there. I shot my arms out to try to catch myself, and my tray slammed onto the floor, and I fell onto it, full force.

A sudden burst of laughter, screeches, then silence. When I got to my knees, the pizza slices came up with me, stuck to my shirt like they'd been glued on. Milk from the smashed carton trickled down my sleeves. "Gross!" somebody said. Another person said, "I've got milk in my *hair!*"

Mrs. Moffett sent someone to get the janitor. Then she looked at me, and sent someone else to the office. "Get the key to the storeroom," she said. Jenna and another girl helped clean up the mess, while I stood by the wastebasket, picking cheese off my shirt. My hands shook. I couldn't speak; I could barely breathe. I didn't want to look at anyone.

"It's all right," Mrs. Moffett said. "Come with me, we'll get you something else to wear."

"This is brand-new," I whispered. The middle school uniform for girls was a plaid polyester skirt and a white polo shirt. Pizza sauce would never come off that shirt. I wondered how much the uniforms cost. I had two sets: That was supposed to be enough. My dad was miffed about all the back-to-school clothes they'd already bought for public school.

In the storeroom, a set of shelves held extra uniforms for sale. Mine had come from there the day before. Mrs. Moffett switched on the light, and shut the door with us both inside. "Take those off," she said. "What size are you?"

No way was I showing my new teacher my bra and underwear. I stood speechless.

"What size?"

"My parents said I could only have two uniforms. They're gonna be mad."

Mrs. Moffett looked thoughtful. "Bring the uniform

you haven't worn yet back tomorrow. We'll exchange it for something you can wear now." When I didn't say anything, she added, "The shirts bleach really well."

I still didn't say anything. Mrs. Moffett sighed, reached over, and checked the size on the label of my shirt. She pulled a shirt and skirt off the shelves, crisp in their plastic bags, and handed them to me. "Get changed, then come back to class."

When I got back, I slid into my chair as quietly as I could. I didn't look at anyone. No one said anything to me. Nearly everyone had finished eating. On the center of my desk sat two baby carrot sticks, washed clean. I ate them.

Jenna said, "Mrs. Moffett, she didn't get lunch."

"Oh, right," said Mrs. Moffett. "Well, after I've gotten the rest of you into church, we'll see if there's any pizza left."

Somebody muttered, "There's never any pizza left."

The boy sitting beside me shoved his tray onto my desk. It still held a big slice. "Go ahead," he said. "I haven't touched it."

When I didn't move, he added, "I don't want it. I never eat all three slices."

I looked up. He was small and wiry, with a bunch of light brown hair that fell in front of his eyes. Pale eyes, olive skin. He bounced a little in his chair. I didn't know his name, but I'd already learned he was always in motion.

"Eat it," he said.

I looked down. The pizza was stone cold by now, the

18

cheese hard and rubbery. But I was starving. "Thanks," I said.

The boy grinned. He waved one hand theatrically, then bowed from the waist, elegantly, even though he was sitting on a chair. "I'm Chris," he said. "Chris Brashares. Happy to be of service, my lady."

CHAPTER

3

One minute later Chris was sticking his tongue out at a boy across the room and crossing his eyes. "Chris," Mrs. Moffett said, "settle down."

She'd told him to settle down three or four thousand times already that day. Chris never settled down. Talk about not being invisible. You couldn't walk into the classroom and not notice Chris. I knew I'd have to stay away from him.

Church was weird. I'd meant it when I told the priest I didn't believe in God. I guess my *parents* might possibly believe in God, but if they did, they'd never told me. I'd never been inside a church before.

There were long seats all around a half circle, in rows with aisles breaking them into sections. In the center of the seats a higher spot held a table and some chairs. Behind the table, above the chairs, hung a great big cross with a statue of Jesus hanging on it. I knew that much, that the statue was supposed to be Jesus. Score one point for me.

Turned out there were a lot of points on the church test, and recognizing Jesus was the only one I got. There was a big sink of water at the back, where we came in. Some of the kids dipped their hands in it, and wiped their foreheads off. I tried it. "You don't have to do that," Jenna whispered, "but if you're going to do it, do it right."

"What's right?"

"You're supposed to cross yourself."

"Oh." I didn't know what she meant. I waited for her to show me, but Mrs. Moffett motioned me toward one of the seats.

Then some people kneeled, and some didn't, and then everybody sat down. Then we all stood up, and sang a song, but it seemed to be one everyone else knew by heart, because no one opened a songbook. The priest came in—Father Micah, the same one I'd met, only wearing an elaborate sort of poncho—along with a boy and a girl who were both wearing robes. "What are they?" I asked Jenna. "Priests in training?"

"Abigail, be quiet," said Mrs. Moffett.

Then everybody sat, and I didn't expect it, so I was the last one down. Then Father Micah said something, and everyone said something back, but I didn't catch it. Then everyone stood up, and I wasn't ready. The whole hour was like that. At one point Father Micah talked for a long time. He was less boring than I expected. Instead of standing behind the podium, he walked up and down in front of the first seats, and he asked a lot of questions. The little kids all waved their hands in the air, hoping he'd pick them.

I didn't listen to anything he said.

21

After more prayers, and sitting, kneeling, standing, kneeling again, everyone got up row by row and walked forward. Father Micah and some of the teachers were handing out little pieces of something. Some of the kids took the pieces and put them in their mouths; others just stood there. When my turn came I held up my hands the way I'd seen the others do.

Father Micah paused for a moment, his hands around a big gold cup. Then with one hand he gently pushed my cupped hands down. He raised his hand over my forehead and said, "May the Lord God bless you, in the name of the Father, and of the Son, and of the Holy Spirit, Amen." He waved his hand over my forehead while he spoke.

I waited. He smiled. He put his hand on my shoulder and gently pushed me to one side. I followed Jenna back to the pew.

"What was that about?" I asked.

"Communion," whispered Jenna.

"What's that thing with the food?"

"Abigail," said Mrs. Moffett. "Shh."

On the way out of church I asked Jenna again. "Communion," she said, "is the Body and Blood of Christ."

"Why wouldn't the priest give me any?"

She frowned. "Do you believe it was the Body of Christ?"

22

That was just about the most ludicrous thing I'd ever heard. "Of course not."

She nodded. "That's why. You got a blessing instead."

"They should tell me the rules, I shouldn't have to guess."

"You're right," Jenna said, somewhat to my surprise. "They should."

"It smelled good in there," I said. "Do churches always smell like that?"

Jenna raised a single eyebrow. "You noticed how it smelled?"

I shrugged and looked away. Invisible, that was me. A line from one of the songs went through my head. It wasn't a whole line really, more of a phrase. *Immortal, invisible, God only wise . . .* If Jenna thought it odd that I'd noticed how the church smelled, I could just imagine what she'd think if I asked questions about the songs.

After church I felt so tired that I couldn't listen to the next class at all. Mrs. Moffett gave out a homework assignment, but I wasn't paying attention and I missed it. She didn't write it on the board either. I wondered if I should care. Instead, I put my head on my desk. I was half asleep when Jenna jogged my arm.

"Wake up," she said. "Time for electives."

Right. Drama. I hoped it was a class I could sleep through.

The drama classroom was big and empty except for chairs and some long, skinny tables. I followed Jenna to the back row and sat down beside her. The room was noisy. I didn't recognize very many of the kids; there were seventh and eighth graders as well as sixth. The teacher stood in front, trying to call roll and shouting for order.

"Helene Antikazides!" the teacher shouted.

"Here!"

"Dominic, you here today?"

"Over here, Mrs. Sumner!"

"I see Mary Hannah, Jenna, Rob. Chris. Where's Chris?"

"Mrs. Sumner, I'd never miss drama," Chris—Chris from my class, Chris who gave me pizza—said from the front row. He sounded so sincere, I expected people to laugh. No one did.

Inexplicably the room grew quiet. Mrs. Sumner beamed at the class. "Today we welcome a new student, Abigail Lorenzo," she said. "Let's say hi to Abigail!"

The drama class applauded.

I looked down at my hands.

"Have you acted before, Abigail?"

I heard the words, but it seemed to be a long time before my brain made sense of them. After what felt like hours, I shook my head.

"Well, don't worry. Everyone's a beginner sometime."

The noise level in the classroom was creeping up again, but Mrs. Sumner clapped her hands, and the room went quiet. "Mimes!" she said. "I want to see your homework. Class, be ready to guess."

I'd seen a mime once and thought he was creepy, with his white-painted face and gloved hands. Clowns scared me, and mimes looked a lot like clowns. No one here did anything with makeup or a costume. They just walked to the open space in front of the class and started acting something out without words or props. We were all supposed to guess what they were.

Some were obvious, and some weren't. One girl spent a lot of time flipping her hair around, and I don't think it was part of her acting. She just naturally flipped her hair all the time, and she couldn't quit doing it. When she was finished, we were supposed to guess her actions. I heard Chris mutter, "You've got a bug in your hair, and you can't get it out."

The girl heard him and glared. "I'm vacuuming," she said.

"Do you always flip your hair when you vacuum?"

"You forgot to turn the vacuum cleaner on."

"What kind of vacuum cleaner was it supposed to be?"

Nobody really liked vacuum girl.

Jenna got up, and surprised me. She stood at one end of the open space, and suddenly her face lifted and became full of light. She called to something—called with her whole body, though she didn't make a sound—and as you watched her face, you swore that someone was running toward her. Then she stepped forward and opened a gate. The gate wasn't real but I could see it. Jenna took a halter off a hook

25

on the fence line and carefully haltered the horse that had run to her. She patted him and gave him a treat on the palm of her hand.

I could see the horse. I could practically smell the horse. I thought how much I'd underestimated Jenna.

When she sat back down, I leaned toward her. "That was great," I whispered.

"Thanks."

Now it was Chris's turn. He stood in front of the class balanced on the balls of his feet, radiating energy. He waited . . . waited . . . and then he dove to the left so hard I couldn't believe the carpet didn't rip his skin. He rolled on the ground, his arms cradling something, then stood and booted it away.

I said, "A soccer goalie."

I didn't realize I'd said it aloud. Chris froze, then flashed a grin at me and bounced back to his seat.

Mrs. Sumner said, "Very good, Abigail! Why don't you go next?"

I went still. I looked at the floor. I said, "I don't know how. I didn't get anything ready."

"That's fine," Mrs. Sumner said. "Just stand up and give it a shot. Use your imagination."

I stood up. I walked to the center of the open space, and I turned to face the class.

I didn't move. I couldn't. I looked up, and saw all their faces, looking at me. My breath came tight in my throat. I could feel myself blushing, feel a hot red wave washing over my skin. My hands shook.

I didn't speak. Didn't move. Couldn't.

After a moment Mrs. Sumner said, "It's okay, Abigail. You can sit down."

I sat down. I put my head on my desk and folded my arms around it, and I didn't move until the bell rang, and my first day at St. Catherine's was over.

CHAPTER
4

On the way out the door Mrs. Sumner stopped me. "I'm sorry," she said.

All I wanted was to get out of that room. "It's fine," I said.

"It's not fine. I should have given you time to think. I shouldn't have sprung something like that on you on your first day here. I'm sorry. Please forgive me."

Too much sympathy and I might fall apart. "I said it was fine!" I growled. I flounced my hair as hard as the vacuum girl had and flung myself out of the room.

I had to go to after-school care, now that I was no longer responsible enough to stay home alone. The after-care teachers herded all of us leftovers together—middle-schoolers, grade-schoolers, and kindergartners—and sent us to the playground. The little kids played on the swing set. The bigger boys played football in the grass. I saw Chris among them, and turned my head away.

On the bench under one of the big trees all the middle-school girls sat together. There weren't very many of them. I recognized one of the girls from drama.

I couldn't go near them, not after what had happened

in the class. I walked around the edge of the playground fence until I found a quiet corner. I sat on the grass with my back against the wall, took my books out of my backpack, and did all my homework except the assignment I hadn't written down.

❧

The next day in drama class I sat in the far back seat in the corner. I pulled out a paperback book and I read all through class. I wore my invisibility cloak. Nobody seemed to notice. In the front of the room the mime show continued. It was mostly very quiet, since mimes don't talk. It was very peaceful, very calm. I could have been anywhere. I could have been back at my old school, with my old friends.

❧

At home the tension made the air thick. After ignoring me for a year and a half my parents now made me the center of attention: Abigail, Exhibit A. They watched me, and watched each other watch me, and wiggle-waggled their eyebrows at each other. "So how's school?" my mother said in a fake cheerful voice.

"Pretty good," I said. "I haven't attacked anyone yet."

"Abigail," she said sharply, "that's not what I meant."

But it *was* what she meant. Everybody kept focusing on what I did to Brett McAvery. No one talked about what he did to me.

My father has a book on his bedside table. *Understanding Your Troubled Child.* I am Troubled. The part that makes me laugh is the idea that he actually wants to Understand me. Because he could have, if he wanted to. If he'd asked questions a week ago, instead of shouting. If he'd listened.

Invisible was safe. "No one pays much attention to me," I told my mother, and she relaxed, because that was the answer she was hoping for.

I wondered what would happen if St. Catherine's expelled me. Homeschooling would be such an attractive option for two people as work-addicted as my parents. They'd have to do more than pay tuition. They'd have to actually deal with me. More likely I'd end up at the alternative school.

"Made any friends yet?" my father asked.

I shrugged.

"Abigail? I'm talking to you."

I shrugged again. I would make a good mime.

CHAPTER

5

I kept my head down. I did my work. No one messed with me. I didn't make friends, didn't talk to anyone, not even Chris or Jenna. The whole week went by without a disaster. On Friday afternoon when I walked through the hallways I felt like I could breathe.

❧

The next Monday Mrs. Sumner took my book out of my hand as I walked into drama. "Sit in the front row," she said. "Time to rejoin the living."

I slouched into the front row. Jenna slouched beside me. The room filled, and everyone was noisy. Chris turned a cartwheel and nearly decked Mrs. Sumner. She shushed everyone until she was about to lose her temper, then suddenly the room went quiet.

"Improvisational mime," she said. "You picked the situations last time, this time it's my turn. In pairs." She held up a bucket. "I've put situations on these pieces of paper. Pick one and go. Chris, you start."

Chris jumped up, and I lifted my head enough to watch him.

"And Abby," Mrs. Sumner said. "Chris and Abby. Go."

I didn't want to, but I stumbled to my feet. Mrs. Sumner held the bucket high, and I reached in and grabbed one of the folded pieces of paper. Chris looked over my shoulder as I read it.

Getting sent to the principal's office.

You had to be kidding me.

"I'll be the principal," Chris whispered. "You come in." He walked to the front of the room and sat down in a chair.

I'd think it was a setup if I hadn't drawn the paper out myself. Part of my brain froze solid. My stomach churned.

But somehow the part of my brain that controlled my feet propelled me forward. Chris pretended to do paperwork. I walked toward the imaginary office door with my head hanging, just right. I opened the door and slunk inside. Chris stood up, a stern expression on his face. He pointed to a second chair, and I sat. I tried to fold my trembling hands on my lap. I tucked my feet neatly beneath the chair and looked up. Chris started to tell me off. He didn't actually speak, of course, but he pointed his finger at me, and shook his head, and mimed yelling at me. I knew he thought it was all my fault.

Except it wasn't. He didn't know the whole story. He should have known, he should have listened, but he didn't. My hands flew up, I tried to explain, and Chris kept ignoring me. He shouted me down—silently—his face full of fury.

32

I stood up. I started to feel furious, the same sort of raging fury that got me expelled. Chris came toward me, still yelling. His face dissolved and I saw Mr. McAvery's face instead, saw him not the last time I was in his office, but the first, and the second, when I felt so scared but sat there anyway, and told him the truth, and actually thought he would believe me and help. Chris didn't give in. He pushed toward me, and anger buzzed through my head, and I pulled my hand back and slapped him, actually slapped him, just as hard as I could.

Chris fell sideways, and his eyes popped open in surprise. I froze. I couldn't believe what I'd done. It was all going to happen again; I was going to be thrown out. Mrs. Sumner was going to call my parents and I'd have nowhere to go. I couldn't breathe.

But the room erupted in laughter. Chris leaped to his feet laughing hardest of all. "Geez!" he said. "Someone needs to teach you stage fighting, girl! You're not supposed to actually *hit* me!"

A bright red mark burned on his cheek, I'd hit him so hard. I opened my mouth to apologize, but what came out, incredibly, was a laugh. Suddenly I was laughing so hard, I couldn't speak. I looked at Mrs. Sumner, and she was laughing, and at Jenna, and she was laughing too. I didn't know why hitting Chris was funny, but everyone thought it was.

Only a tiny bit of me actually found it funny. If I wasn't

careful, I'd quit laughing and start to sob. I wiped my eyes and took a deep breath. It was hard, keeping myself together.

"Next," Mrs. Sumner said. "Jacob and Morgan. Go."

I returned to my seat. My hands still shook a little. I felt like something had cracked open inside me, but maybe, just maybe, it was a good kind of crack, not a bad one. I almost felt like a person again.

☙

Mid-term reports went home just a week and a half later. My parents seemed surprised. "All A's!" my father said. "Right across the board. Quite a nice improvement, Abigail."

My mother looked. "Is St. Catherine's easy?" she asked. "Of course, I suppose you haven't had time for too much."

"Smaller class sizes," my father said. "More attention. Good. Nice to know that tuition pays for something."

My mother smiled at me. "Well, good. I'm glad you're working hard." She took a bite of her grilled chicken salad. It was a Wednesday night, which meant it was Family Night, our grand look-at-us-all-eating-dinner-together night. Ever since my mom didn't make partner at her law firm, a year ago, she'd stayed late at the office almost every night. Wednesday dinners were supposed to make up for her missing Mondays, Tuesdays, Thursdays, and Fridays. Dad and I ate a lot of take-out food.

"Hey," my father said, "if you're actually so smart, how come you didn't do this well before?"

My mother's eyes widened. I froze; my food stuck like a lump in my throat. "I d-d-did," I stammered, swallowing hard. "In third grade. And fourth. Before . . . you know."

He paused. "I was joking," he said. "Don't look like that. It was a joke."

"How could that be a joke?" I asked.

He didn't answer. I waited, looking at him. My mom looked at him too. He cleared his throat. "I'm sorry, honey," he said. "Sometimes . . . well, you're right, I shouldn't joke. I know you're smart." He looked away from me, back to my mid-term marks. "And look, you even got an A in religion. What's that like?"

"What's what like?"

"You know." He chuckled. "Religion. Catholics. What do you think of them?"

As though Catholics were a separate species. I felt a surge of anger. "I like them," I said. "The way they're so holy and all."

My father's eyebrows shot up. "Holy?" he repeated.

"Yeah," I said, innocently poking around in my salad. "You know. Like how they love Jesus so much and pray all the time and everything."

The only people at St. Catherine's I knew for sure were Catholic were Jenna and Chris. I couldn't imagine them praying, ever, unless some priest or teacher told them they had to, and I didn't have the faintest idea whether or not they loved Jesus, but I could see that the idea of loving Jesus irritated my Dad. "I wish I were more like that," I said.

Suddenly my dad was absolutely not joking. "You don't need to be any different than you are," he said. "You're fine."

"Completely fine," my mother said.

Except for that little episode in the cafeteria. Except for how I felt, which was anything but fine. "If I was fine," I said, "I wouldn't be at St. Catherine's."

For once, just once, I wished we could talk about what happened. I wished we could talk about everything.

Mom and Dad threw a couple of looks back and forth at each other. I didn't know what the looks meant. "Well," my dad said, getting up from the table. "That was a great dinner. I've got to make a few phone calls."

Mom kissed me on the cheek. "You'll clear the table, okay, honey?" She got up and left the room too.

I sat at the table, twirling my fork in my hands. That's what I would do, I thought, to really get under my parents' skin. I'd become Catholic. They'd go nuts.

CHAPTER
6

At lunch I usually sat with Jenna and her crowd. I wasn't exactly friends with them, but I wasn't not-friends either, which was good enough. Thursday's lunch was taco salad, one of my favorites. "I want to be Catholic," I said. "How do I do it?"

Jenna rolled her eyes at me. "You? You sleep through church."

"I got an A in religion."

"Anyone with half a brain gets an A in religion."

"How do I do it?"

"First," Jenna said, "you believe in God."

She had me there, though I don't know how she knew it. "Fine," I said. "What's second?"

A girl named Chelsea spoke up. "You have to go to classes. Every Wednesday night until Easter. My Dad did it a couple of years ago."

Better and better. I'd escape Family Night.

"Great. Where do I sign up for the classes?"

They shrugged. "Are you serious?" Jenna asked.

"Sure."

"Huh."

It was raining, so we were stuck inside for after-care, crammed into a second-grade classroom on the first floor. Chris took out a handful of rubber bands and shot them at the after-care teacher, one at a time, from around the corner of a bookcase. The teacher couldn't quite catch him at it.

"Hey," I said, sitting down on the floor beside him.

"Hey," he said. He peeked around the edge of the bookcase and fired another rubber band. I heard it smack something. The teacher yelled. Chris dove back to the ground, giggling.

"Chris!" the teacher said. "I want to see you doing home-work right now."

Chris rolled onto his back and dragged his backpack closer. He pulled out a book, opened it, then shot another rubber band.

"I'm going to become Catholic," I said.

The after-care teacher marched over. "Show me your hands."

"What?" said Chris.

"Show 'em."

Chris held up his empty hands with an air of injured innocence. The teacher rolled her eyes and walked away. "Got any rubber bands?" he asked me.

"Didn't you hear what I just said?"

38

"Yeah. You're going to be Catholic. Are you serious?"

"Yep. It'll really tick my parents off."

He laughed. "Cool."

"Chelsea said I have to take classes. You know anything about that?"

"Yeah, sure." He dug through his backpack and came up with more rubber bands. "My mom sponsored somebody once. Maybe she can sponsor you." He popped off another rubber band. The teacher looked up in time to see it.

"You," she said. "Out in the hallway. Now."

"I don't want to get your mom involved," I called as the teacher frog-marched him out of the room. That would be taking it too seriously.

"You can't do it by yourself," he called back. The teacher said something I couldn't hear. "We were having a *conversation*," he said back. His voice faded as he went down the hall.

♃

The next day in after-care Chris came up to me. "What'd you hit me for?" he asked.

"What?"

"You know. You hit me. In class."

"You thought it was funny."

"That isn't why you did it."

"I was acting," I said.

"No," he said. "You weren't. Why'd you hit me?"

I flushed. I could feel my pulse speed up. But nobody else was listening; it was just me and Chris, behind the bookcase. I said, "It was like talking to . . . It was like being right back in my old middle school. I didn't mean it."

Chris snorted. "You hit pretty hard for somebody who didn't mean it."

"Yeah, well—"

He cut me off. "Why'd you get kicked out?"

"Don't know."

"Duh," he said. "Of course you do."

"Assault."

He rolled onto his stomach and looked up at me. His eyes were a funny color, blue and gray and green all at the same time. "Seriously? You're, like, the quietest person in this school."

"Yep."

"And you got kicked out for *assault*?"

"That's what they called it."

He didn't say anything for a few minutes. "What'd you assault with?" he asked at last.

"A Swiss Army knife."

His eyes opened wider. "Guess I'm glad you didn't have a knife in drama class."

"They took it away from me," I said.

"No kidding."

"It was my cousin's idea," I said. "My older cousin, Debbie, she lives in Ohio and she goes to college. We

were at my nana's house last Thanksgiving and I was telling her about the stuff that was happening at my school,
with this one boy, and she said I should stand up for myself."

"Your *cousin* thought you should stab somebody?"

"Well, not exactly. But she said something like that
had happened to her once, and she said I shouldn't let
anybody hurt me. So I bought a knife. With my babysitting
money."

Chris's mouth hung open.

"I wish I still had it," I said. "I felt safer when I had a
knife."

"Jesus," said Chris.

"Right," I said. "Exactly." Though what the knife had to
do with Jesus I couldn't say.

He shook his head, and I thought he was about to say
something else, but three of the fourth graders came up
then and challenged Chris to a game of tabletop football. I
turned my back to them, and after a moment Chris walked
away. I tucked myself into a corner behind some bookcases
and tried to do my science homework, but I couldn't con-
centrate. My stomach clenched and rolled. For a moment
I'd made myself visible. Visible was bad.

41

CHAPTER
7

For a week or so I went back to keeping my head down, my thoughts to myself. Chris didn't try to have a conversation with me again, and I wondered if I'd scared him away. I hadn't thought Chris would scare easily. He got in trouble almost every day, and it never seemed to bother him. He argued with teachers. He talked all the time. Even when he was quiet, he was nearly always moving. His fingers flicked against his desktop, or his feet shuffled, or he bounced in his chair.

I could sit motionless for hours.

It was October. October was the Month of the Rosary, although no one seemed to know why. When I asked, Mrs. Moffett frowned and didn't answer. I frowned back. I disliked arbitrary things.

"Does anyone here not know what the rosary is?" Mrs. Moffett asked.

I raised my hand. I was the only one. I guessed that the other non-Catholics had been here in October before.

The rosary was actually fifty-five prayers said all in a row. Most of them, Mrs. Moffett told us, were Hail Marys. A rosary was a thing like a bead necklace that you used to keep track of the Hail Marys, because it was hard to count to fifty-five and pray at the same time. You said a Hail Mary on each little bead, and something else on bigger beads, and it didn't mean anything to me because I'd never heard of any of the prayers. They weren't ever said in the Mass. I raised my hand. "What's a Hail Mary?"

Mrs. Moffett started to look annoyed, then realized that I wasn't being a smart aleck, I really didn't know. She looked in the back of our religion book, but the prayer wasn't there. "Just follow along as best you can," she said.

Then, honest to God, we actually prayed a rosary. Out loud. The whole class. It took half an hour, all the rest of religion period. The Hail Marys sounded like, "Hail Mary, mumble, mumble, the Lord is Swiss cheese." I didn't think that was right, but it was what it sounded like.

"Do you know the Hail Mary?" I asked my father at dinner.

"The football pass?" he said.

"No," I said, "the rosary prayer."

"Ah," he said. "No. I don't."

"I have to look it up for homework," I said. "So I can learn how to pray the rosary."

He started to say something, but my mother interrupted to tell me I could use her computer. They both looked worried. I'd been making myself invisible and had half forgotten how worked up I could get them by seeming to take religion seriously.

I didn't really have to look up the Hail Mary. Mrs. Moffett

hadn't seemed to care. But I couldn't get "the Lord is Swiss cheese" out of my mind. I went online and typed in *www. Catholicprayers.com,* and got a Catholic singles dating service. No kidding. Like a nice Catholic boy would be the answer to my prayers.

I tried again on Google and found a site.

> *Hail Mary, full of grace, the Lord is with thee.*
> *Blessed are you among women, and blessed is the fruit*
>   *of your womb, Jesus.*
> *Holy Mary, Mother of God, pray for us sinners now*
>   *and at the hour of our death. Amen.*

That was it. No Swiss cheese, which was a relief. But I didn't see why it was so important. I had expected something more interesting. Also nothing on the Web site explained why the rosary was in October.

I decided to ask Father Micah. At lunch I went downstairs to find him, and the secretary told me to wait on the bench outside the offices.

Chris was already sitting there, tapping his feet, tap, tap, tap, till the noise started echoing in my head.

"Please stop that," I said.

He kept tapping. "Stab anyone today?"

"No," I said. "Have you?"

A week had gone by without anyone saying anything to me about knives, stabbings, or assault, so I knew Chris hadn't blabbed.

"I should've," Chris said. "It wasn't my fault this time."

I'd heard Chris say that before. "It's never your fault," I said.

He turned toward me, his eyes glinting. "Most of the time it really isn't," he said.

"I know." I'd seen teachers blame Chris for other kids' stuff. He was easy to blame. He was usually doing something wrong, it was just something smaller than what he actually got blamed for.

"What's the point of behaving," he said, "when you're going to get in trouble anyway?"

Ms. Jackson, the principal, opened her door. She waved Chris into her office with a tired expression on her face. She paused when she saw me. "Just me," Chris said. "Abby's not in trouble."

"I'm waiting to talk to Father Micah," I said.

I had learned that Father Micah was not actually the school principal; he was the parish priest. Ms. Jackson had been out of town the day I came for my school interview.

After a few minutes the secretary told me Father Micah could see me now. When I got to his office door I was suddenly too nervous to step inside. He looked up at me and smiled. "Come in," he said, gesturing to an empty chair.

I stayed in the doorway. "What's the deal with October being the Month of the Rosary?"

"October seventh is the Feast of Our Lady of the Rosary," he said, without a single pause to think about it, much less look it up in a book. "On that day we remember Mary and the rosary at Mass. It dates back to the Middle Ages, when the rosary first developed as a prayer."

"October seventh is a Monday," I said. "We don't have Mass on Mondays."

"The school doesn't," he said. "I do. Some of the parishioners come to Mass every day."

It seemed meaningless, the way most of religion seemed meaningless—just lists of stuff to memorize. That afternoon we had a test on the Mysteries of the Rosary, the Sorrowful, Joyful, and Glorious, and the Mysteries of Light. I aced it. I can memorize with the best of them.

It was a shame, I thought, that the stuff we learned in religion class was so far away from the sounds and smells that permeated the church. I'd gotten comfortable enough with the school Mass routine that there were actually parts I looked forward to. At the close of one really long prayer, when we were all on our knees, Father Micah held up a big Communion wafer and sang the ending of the prayer in a round, bell-like voice. I loved the singing. It sent this feeling of peace over the whole school; even the kindergartners stopped squirming in their seats and the fourth graders stopped whispering and passing notes.

It was the one part of church everyone listened to.

I liked the listening feeling. But October being the Month of the Rosary, well, that made about as much sense as the Lord is Swiss cheese.

Drama was short skits now. We had actual parts—more stuff to memorize. Most of the skits were incredibly stupid, but it was still easy to tell who was good at drama and who wasn't.

Only a few boys took drama, but they were all good. They flung their arms wide when they talked, and jumped around, and filled up the little space in the front of the room so thoroughly that I never felt I could move when I was up there with them. I envied the way they needed so much room, the way they seemed to want an audience instead of being afraid.

About half the girls were good; the rest stunk. Some stunk because they were there for the same reason I was: because drama seemed like the least academic elective. Others, like Jenna's friend Rachel, signed up just so they could hang out with their friends. Rachel never bothered to learn her lines, and she drove Mrs. Sumner crazy.

"This is an *assignment,* Rachel," she said one afternoon, waving a script in the air. Mrs. Sumner was very dramatic. "You are getting a *grade* on how well you perform this skit. Learning your lines is *not* optional. You *have* to do it."

I was in a boring skit about a cat. Rachel's skit was about eating spaghetti, and was funny, or at least it should have been. Between Rachel not knowing any of her lines, and Helene reciting hers like she was reading the phone book, it never sounded funny. I knew it should have.

The third day that Helene and Rachel stumbled through the not-funny spaghetti skit, Chris lost his mind entirely. "No! No!" he shouted, leaping from his seat. "It's supposed to be funny!" Chris wasn't fooling around; he looked furious. "Like this!" He said Helene's first line—and he said it right, and people laughed.

Rachel got out almost half of the next line before she stumbled.

"You've never had spaghetti like my mother makes it." I surprised myself by speaking aloud. Rachel's head spun around. She glared at me.

Chris jumped in with Helene's line. I got to my feet and said Rachel's. We traded it back and forth, and did the whole skit without a mistake, and although it wasn't as funny as it could have been if we had worked on it, it was a whole lot better than anything Helene and Rachel ever did.

I laughed. Chris laughed. Rachel crossed her arms and sulked.

"Sit *down*," Mrs. Sumner said. "Chris, Abby, both of you." I scurried to my seat. Chris didn't move. His eyes sparked.

"If she's so ignorant—"

48

"*Sit!*" I've never heard Mrs. Sumner use such a sharp tone. Chris sat. He covered his face with his hands. When it was time for his skit he performed it as well as always, but his eyes still looked furious. I wasn't sure why he was so angry.

When class finished Mrs. Sumner told Chris to stay. I spilled half the stuff out of my backpack on purpose and put it back very, very slowly so I could hear.

Mrs. Sumner sat beside Chris. "Good actors don't grandstand," she said quietly. There wasn't a trace of anger left in her voice. "I know you know everyone else's lines as well as your own. I know you're more talented than Helene." Chris snorted. Mrs. Sumner continued. "If we asked her, she'd probably say she knows it too. That doesn't matter. It's her part, not yours."

"But she didn't—"

"Doesn't matter," Mrs. Sumner said. "I'm the director. It's up to me who gets what part. It's not up to you. Go on now to after-school."

Chris stomped out the door without looking up. "You too, Abby," Mrs. Sumner said. "Everything I said to Chris goes for you too."

I tried to slink invisibly away.

CHAPTER

8

In after-care Chris sat on a bench on the playground, played his Game Boy, and ignored everyone, including me. I didn't know why he was so upset. I couldn't tell if he was mad at Mrs. Sumner for telling him off, or still mad at Helene for basic incompetence. Or was he somehow angry with me? I nearly walked over and asked him, but I'd blown my cover enough for one day.

At dinner, though, I was still puzzling over it, and made the mistake of mentioning it to my parents. My father pointed his fork at me. "Keep away from him," he said. "The last thing you need is more trouble over a boy."

"This isn't anything like last year," I said. "Chris isn't—"

"It's not last year I'm worried about," said my father. "Last year was fine. It was the beginning of this year that was the problem."

That was not true. It was so completely not true. All of last year was the heart of the problem. I couldn't believe my parents still didn't understand. I felt utter despair.

"We know what happened was an aberration, Abigail," Mom said. "We know you're not really like that. We want to put what happened behind us, and we want school to go well for you, so of course we don't want you mixed up with the wrong kind of people."

"Chris isn't the wrong kind of people," I said.

"It sounds like he could be," my father said. "You're much better off being careful."

"I was careful before. It didn't help."

Silence. Nothing. I was never more invisible to my parents than when I tried to talk about Brett McAvery.

Chris couldn't be more different from Brett. He was loud, obvious, in-your-face. Brett was sneaky. Brett thought scaring me was fun.

Was what happened an aberration? Or would I, in the same situation, do it again? Aberrant Abigail, that was me.

℞

I understood more of the Mass now. Jenna had showed me where the responses were written in the front of the hymnbook, so I mostly knew what to say when. I had the stand up/sit down/kneel stuff all figured out. I knew how to cross myself correctly. I mostly listened to the Bible readings, and I tried to pay attention to the homily, which was the official name for the sermon.

I could do the whole Mass thing, it just still didn't make much sense. I kept feeling like it *should* make sense, but it didn't. Except for those odd moments. Most of the time I had stuff constantly running through my head—school stuff, or things I had to memorize, or, if I wasn't careful, memories of Brett and of stabbing him and of the panicky, suffocating way I'd felt—but once in a while, in the church, my whole mind got quiet. My body was always quiet, so it wasn't like I went into a trance or anything. It wasn't a difference anyone could see. But I felt better for a few minutes. It felt like peace.

Mrs. Moffett was Catholic; she took Communion at Mass. She was also a pretty good teacher, and didn't seem mean. One day I hung back at the end of school and asked her what I should do if I wanted to become Catholic. I thought she'd look surprised, but she didn't so much as raise an eyebrow. "Go talk to Father Micah," she said. "He'll tell you."

☙

This time I made an appointment, for the next day right after school. When I knocked on Father Micah's open door he was sitting at his desk with his back to the window, reading. He got up, smiling, and shook my hand. He seemed gentle. I was so nervous, I could barely breathe. I guess he still seemed a lot like a principal to me.

"Sit down," he said, pointing at a chair.

I stayed standing, my schoolbooks clutched to my chest like a shield. "I want to be Catholic," I said.

He gestured again to the chair. "Please, sit down." His voice was very calm. I sat. I put my books on my lap. "You want to become Catholic," he said.

"Yes." I waited for him to ask if I believed in God. After all, I had told him that I didn't on the first day of school.

"Why?" he asked instead.

To tick my parents off. "I don't really know," I said. Father Micah waited, still looking at me. I fidgeted and looked away. He had photos on his desk, smiling family photos. I wondered who the people in them were.

"I guess I feel called," I whispered. Wasn't that a holy sort of thing? To be called? I considered telling him about the peace feeling, but it seemed too much like a real reason, like I was trying to be serious about it. Better to tick my parents off than to flirt with actually believing.

"I see," he said. "What do your parents think about it?"

"I haven't told them," I said. He waited, and I added, because I couldn't help myself, "They're going to hate it."

"And this is okay with you?" he asked.

"Yes." The word came out as a hiss, full of so much anger that it startled me. But I was an actor, I thought. I did pretty well in drama; I wasn't useless there. I cleared my throat and tried again, in a softer voice. "I mean—no. I wish they'd be okay with it. I don't think they will be. They're not really Jesus people."

"And you, are you a Jesus person?" His eyebrows were raised. He didn't look skeptical so much as genuinely curious.

"I don't know much about Jesus," I said. So much for

53

acting; I kept telling the truth. "But I'd like to learn more." Where did that come from? I didn't want to know more. Not making a fool of myself in Mass was enough for me.

"Good," said Father Micah. He got up and opened a closet door, and came back holding a chunky paperback book, which he handed to me. It was a Bible. "Here's where you start. The New Testament is all about Jesus."

I didn't know what I expected him to give me—maybe a secret Catholic decoder ring, or some sort of special badge for Catholics, or something like that—but it wasn't a Bible. I opened it. The pages were paper-thin, the print impossibly small. "Thanks," I said.

"When you've read a little, come back and talk again," Father Micah said.

"Okay." I stood up, and was halfway to the door when I turned around. "It's because I'm a kid, isn't it? That you won't let me get started right away? I have to have my parents' permission." Which I'll never get.

Father Micah smiled. "Becoming Catholic is a commitment for a lifetime," he said. "Never something to enter into in a hurry. New members receive sacraments and join the church at Easter, and the period between Advent and Easter is used for discernment and preparation."

It was barely Halloween. Easter was months away. "What's Advent?" I said.

"The four weeks preceding Christmas," he said. "The

word *Advent* means 'waiting.' Discernment and preparation means you listen to find out what God truly calls you to do, and you figure out how to do it. And you don't need your parents' permission—anyone over age seven is old enough to choose for herself." He paused. "Start with the Bible. It's a good first step."

CHAPTER

9

Halloween came and went, and then we had auditions for a Christmas play. Mrs. Moffett passed scripts out to everyone. It was about a boy and a girl who tried to stay up late to wait for Santa, but ended up discovering the true meaning of Christmas—Jesus—instead. Holy drivel, not something you'd get away with at a public school. At night I read the script over, and felt pleased. It was a stupid play, but I could picture Chris and me in the two main parts. We'd be great. All the next day at school I couldn't wait for auditions.

Mrs. Sumner had moved her desk to the side of the room, and as we walked past it on our way in, she handed us audition forms to fill out. They were very official—she wanted to know our height and weight and special talents and previous experience, as well as what parts we wanted to try for. I didn't have any talents or experience, and Mrs. Sumner could see my height and weight for herself. "What's this?" I asked Chris.

"It's what all the theaters use," he said, as though he'd just auditioned on Broadway and knew all about it. "The theaters around here," he amended. "I had a part in *Annie* last summer."

I remembered seeing an ad about that. So Chris had experience.

The form said to list three parts. I only put down one, the one I wanted, Susie, the girl who stayed up for Santa—and penciled a little star beside it. A lot of the rest of the parts were silly: Christmas Wishes and Night Stars, and angels and gifts, things like that. I didn't want to be any of those.

I fidgeted while the first people got up with their scripts and began to read. None of them seemed good to me.

"Abby," Mrs. Sumner said. I got up and tried to walk to the center of the room confidently, as though I were deserving of the best part possible. "Read starting on page three, the part of the Christmas Cookie." A talking cookie! That's when things started to get strange in the play, when the cookies that had been put out for Santa came to life. "I'd like to read for Susie," I said.

"You can be considered for Susie," she replied. "Read the Cookie part."

I read the Cookie part. It was dumb.

That was it. That was my audition.

I slumped back down between Jenna and Chris. "How stupid," I muttered. They looked at me without saying anything.

Chris got the boy part, all right. Jenna got to be Susie. This was doubly annoying because Jenna was taller than anyone else in the class, including the boys, and she weighed more too. She did not look like a little girl staying up for Santa. I did.

Except—I had to be honest, because Jenna was the closest thing to a friend that I had—Jenna would be able to *act* like a little girl staying up for Santa. She would be able to make the audience think she was a little girl. She'd probably even make them believe the sappy ending, when she was supposed to be transformed by the true spirit of Christmas.

At after-care I complained to Chris about my lousy Cookie role. He didn't look sympathetic like I expected. "Don't let Mrs. Sumner hear you say that," he said. "You'll be stuck with bit parts until you graduate. She hates it when people whine."

"I'm not whining! I'd be really good!"

"Whatever," he said. "Sounds like whining to me."

I grabbed his arm. "Don't you think I'd be good?"

"Probably," he said. He shook my hand off. "We'll never know unless you're decent as a Christmas Cookie. Look, nobody gets a big part their first time out. Mrs. Sumner wants to see how you are with a little one."

"Except you and Jenna," I said, hurt. They were sixth graders, like me, barely into middle school. This was their first show too.

"We do community theater," he said. "So does Mrs. Sumner. We go way back. And anyway," he added, "I didn't want the Sammy part. I wanted to be the Night Wind."

"Bummer," I said, not sorry for him at all.

I had stuck the Bible Father Micah gave me onto my night-stand, conspicuously, where my parents would see it, but of course they hadn't noticed. The night I became a Christmas Cookie I went to bed early, tired and angry, and I picked the Bible up before I turned out my light. Father Micah had said to begin with the New Testament. It took me a while to find it, because there wasn't really a table of contents that made sense to me. But eventually, about two-thirds of the way back, I found the beginning of the Gospel of Matthew, and for all my trouble was rewarded with one giant list of unpronounceable names: ". . . And Rehoboam became the father of Abijah, and Abijah became the father of Asa, and Asa became the father of Jehoshaphat . . ." Like that. Totally meaningless. Probably something I would eventually have to memorize.

Along with a stupid Christmas Cookie part.

I snapped off my light and seethed in the dark.

"Nothing's meaningless," Chris said when I complained about the Bible to him at school the next day. "Just because you don't understand something doesn't make it meaningless."

"Okay," I said, "you explain it."

"I can't explain it," he said. "But I'm not worried about it, either."

"You aren't any fun to complain to," I said.

He looked amazed. "Why should I be fun to complain to?"

Jenna asked what was up. I could hardly tell her I was mad that she got the part I wanted, so I told her about the Bible and the annoying list of names. "Just skip that part," she said. "Skip whatever doesn't make sense."

I supposed I might as well. That night I read about Jesus being born, which I'd pretty much already picked up on, and then about King Herod killing all the baby boys in Bethlehem, which I was amazed I'd never heard about. It seemed like a pretty big deal to only get one little Bible verse. Then I skipped a big chunk about John the Baptist, because, I mean, who cares? And then I got to this:

> *Blessed are the poor in spirit,*
> *for theirs is the kingdom of heaven.*
> *Blessed are those who mourn,*
> *for they shall be comforted.*
> *Blessed are the meek,*
> *for they shall inherit the earth.*
> *Blessed are those who hunger and thirst*
> *for righteousness, for they shall be satisfied.*
> *Blessed are the merciful,*
> *for mercy shall be theirs.*

I could not explain precisely what that meant, but when I

read it, I understood it. It was a peaceful sort of passage, like that feeling in church. A promise—Jesus' promise that life wasn't going to suck forever.

God, I hoped not.

Only where was the part that said *"Blessed are those who assault boys with pocketknives . . ."*? Hungering and thirsting for righteousness didn't sound quite the same as being filled with anger, somehow.

It was important, wasn't it? That I was right and Brett McAvery was wrong? If he hadn't threatened to pull down my pants, I wouldn't have stabbed him. He deserved it.

Didn't he?

CHAPTER
10

I hated being a Christmas Cookie, but, mindful of Chris's warning, attempted to be the best Christmas Cookie I could be.

It wasn't easy. My costume was made of cardboard, shaped like a giant star, and covered with glitter paint. I sparkled.

"Be happy," Chris said. "You're a cookie . . . um, everybody loves you."

"I spend my days on a plate, waiting to be eaten," I said. "What's there to be happy about?"

But I was careful not to complain to Mrs. Sumner, or to anyone other than Chris and Jenna. I memorized my few pathetic lines by the end of the first week, and I delivered them with as much gusto as a piece of pastry should be allowed. I knew my entrances and exits, and, unlike Chris, never rolled my eyes when other people missed theirs. Unlike Joshua, I never tried to make anyone else crack up. I did not make frosting jokes or say I'd rather be a Fig Newton. I was a good cookie.

Two of the Christmas Wishes did complain—constantly, annoyingly, and vehemently, until Mrs. Sumner yanked their crummy parts right away from them and banished them to the Props Committee. They got to paint my Christmas Cookie costume.

I got to be a replacement Christmas Wish.

"Duh," Chris said. "The Cookies are one of the only parts that aren't onstage at the same time as the Wishes. It's not like Mrs. Sumner had a choice."

"It's because I'm a such good cookie," I said. "Don't be jealous."

The Christmas Wish part was not a whole lot less stupid than the Christmas Cookie part, but on the day before Thanksgiving Mrs. Sumner brought in our costumes. "I couldn't think what a Christmas Wish was supposed to look like," she said, "so I just borrowed these. They're from the community theater's *Romeo and Juliet*. What do you think?"

Mine was a red velvet dress with gold lacing and gold trim and wide cuffed sleeves. I loved it. I put it on and twirled around, and the skirt swung out like a red bell.

❦

Every year on Thanksgiving we went to my nana's house in Cleveland. All my cousins were there. Nana died last February, but I knew my aunts and uncles would be eating together somewhere—probably at Aunt Lucy's, because she lived closest to Cleveland. When I'd asked my mom about it, she'd frowned and said, "We thought we'd try something different this year. We thought we'd stay here."

"Why?" I'd asked.

She'd avoided my eye. "Oh, change is nice sometimes. And, you know, Mr. Allister invited us to his house for dinner. Doesn't that sound fun?"

Mr. Allister was the jerk who denied my mother partnership. Mr. Allister was the reason my mom worked so many nights, and almost had a stroke when she had to take time off to deal with my "incident." We were going to spend Thanksgiving sucking up to Mr. Allister.

It was even worse than I feared. When we walked in the door Mr. Allister's wife offered my parents drinks and then looked at me, stunned. "Abigail!" she said. "Oh, I completely forgot about you!"

I looked back at her, equally stunned, unable to believe she'd said that. Hello? Manners? Mrs. Allister sputtered and laughed a little, and then said, "We don't have any soda, dear—nobody here drinks it—would you like a glass of milk?"

"No," I said. My mother shot me a look, so I added, "Thank you. I'll have water with dinner."

After that kind of opening it was hard for me to even pretend I liked being there. It turned out they weren't serving dinner for a couple of hours. No one else brought kids. Almost everyone was older than my parents, so it's possible their children were grown-ups, but still—who ever heard of Thanksgiving without kids? All the women stood in the kitchen, pretending to cook but really just drinking bloody

Marys and gossiping, and I hung around them until my mother whispered, "Didn't you bring something to do?"

"No," I whispered back. "I didn't know I would need something to do *on Thanksgiving*."

I wandered into the other room, where the men were watching football. Mr. Allister looked pretty tipsy. I squeezed next to my dad on the couch. "Hi, sweetie," he said. "This isn't really the place for you, okay?"

"I hear bad words all the time at school," I protested. I thought that was why he wanted me to leave, because some of the men were cussing.

Everyone laughed. My dad turned red. "Nice," he said. "I pay good money to send you to a private school, and you're learning bad language?"

"How's she making out at St. Catherine's, Eddie?" one man asked Dad. "You happy you made the switch?"

Dad put on his solemn face. "You know, we are. The academics are just so much better than at a public school, and Abigail's a bright young lady. She deserves the best."

Maybe I deserved the best—though I doubted my dad thought so—but I wouldn't have been getting it if I hadn't been thrown out of public school. I could tell these people hadn't heard that part of the story.

I got up and stomped back to the kitchen. Mom raised her eyebrows at me.

"I should've brought my script," I muttered. I could have worked on my Christmas Wish lines.

"What script?" asked one of the other women.

"Abigail's taking drama in school," my mother said. "They're putting on a little play."

"It's not little," I said.

"She takes it very seriously," my mother said. "What's your part? A Christmas Cake?"

"A Christmas Cookie," I said. "But now I get to be a Christmas Wish too."

The other women laughed. "Oh, that sounds just like the pageant Kevin did when he was in kindergarten," one said. "It was the cutest little thing!"

I knew being a Christmas Cookie sounded like a baby part. I knew it probably sounded like whatever Kevin did. But I still said, "I wish you all wouldn't keep calling it little. It's pretty big to me."

"Abigail!" my mother said.

Which is how I ended up spending three hours on Thanksgiving Day in the Allisters' deserted family room reading back issues of *Golf Digest* and *Cosmopolitan*. You wouldn't believe the stuff they put in *Cosmopolitan*. I would rather have stayed home alone.

On the way home I asked, "Can one of you please drive me to church on Sunday?"

There was a long silent moment. Then my Dad asked, "What church?"

"St. Catherine's," I said. "You don't have to stay, you could just drop me off and come back for me."

"But honey," my mother said, "Sundays are our rest days."

Mom slept until eleven most Sundays. Dad got up at eight and went for a long run. "I know," I said, "but Dad's usually home by nine. He could drive me to nine-thirty Mass and then come home and shower before picking me up."

"So now you're calling it Mass?" Dad sounded angry.

"It's what it's called," I said.

"Where's this coming from?" Mom asked. "This sudden church thing?"

I considered saying that the only way I could keep my straight-A grades for the semester was by going to church every weekend, but I didn't think it was right to lie about religion. At least, not quite that much. "Please," I said. "It's important." And honestly, I thought my brain was about to

explode after that stupid Thanksgiving, and more than anything I wanted just a tiny bit of peace. Just that part where
Father Micah sang would be enough.

"We'll think about it," my mother said, at the same time
that my Dad said, "No. Don't be silly, Abigail. You don't
need to go to church."

When we got home I yanked the school directory out of
the desk under the phone and called Chris. "Can your mom
give me a ride to church Sunday morning?" I asked.

"Sure," he said, without asking her. "But it'll be the early
Mass, I'm warning you. I've got to be an altar server."

"That's fine."

"How was your Thanksgiving?" he asked.

"Terrible. We spent it with a bunch of moron attorneys
we weren't related to, and all the food was bad. We didn't
even have normal turkey, we had some kind of basil pesto
turkey breast. The stuffing had oysters in it. We had pumpkin
praline cheesecake instead of pumpkin pie."

Chris made a vomiting noise.

"The thing I missed most," I said, "aside from my nana,
and my cousin Debbie, and the rest of my cousins—the food
thing I missed most is that green bean casserole with the
cream soup mixed in."

"Come on over," Chris said. "We've got tons left."

I didn't know where Chris lived, but it turned out to
be close enough that I could ride my bike there. That was
good, because Dad was sleeping on the couch and Mom had

had too many bloody Marys to drive. She was sitting in the wing chair next to the couch, looking fuzzy and limp. "I'm going to a friend's house," I said.

She looked up. "That's nice."

"I'll be home by bedtime," I said.

"Okay." As I was about to leave the room, she added, "That was awful, wasn't it?" I nodded. My mother sighed. "I'm sorry," she said. "We won't do it again."

Chris and his mom lived in a little brick house that was perfectly square. The flower beds in front were filled with dried stalks of what must have been pretty flowers in the summertime, and two uncarved pumpkins flanked the door. I parked my bike on the front walk and rang the bell, suddenly nervous. I'd seen Chris's mom when she picked him up from after-care, but I'd never spoken to her.

Chris opened the door. "Hey," he said. "Come in." He looked happier than I'd ever seen him; he bounced when he walked, but not with the nervous energy he gave off at school. "Got your green beans right here," he said.

When you go in the door of their house you walk straight into the family room. Squishy denim armchairs and a plump sofa surround a big battered coffee table; right then it was covered with used plates and glasses, and Mrs. Brashares was stacking them. "Hi, Abby," she said, as casually as if I always visited. "Happy Thanksgiving."

They had a fire burning in the fireplace. It was a comforting room. "In here, Abby," Chris called from the kitchen.

He'd set a place at the table, with a placemat, napkin, and fork. He handed me a plate with a steaming mound of green bean casserole. "I heated it up in the microwave," he said. "What do you want to drink? Pepsi?"

Chris sat next to me and ate a piece of pumpkin pie, and then I ate pie, and then I had more green bean casserole. "Now I feel like it's Thanksgiving," I said.

Mrs. Brashares began to wash the huge stack of dishes piled by the sink. "Every year, I wonder why I don't switch to paper plates," she said.

"Because it's Thanksgiving," Chris said.

"Because it's Thanksgiving," she agreed. She looked at me. "Half our guests were still here when you called," she said. "They just left. I should have made them wash dishes."

I looked at the pile of dishes, and the tiny kitchen. Pots and pans and casserole dishes covered every inch of countertop.

"I can help," I said.

"Thanks, honey," Mrs. Brashares said. "I'm thinking this can just all wait until tomorrow." She turned out the light above the kitchen sink and went back to the family room. I saw her settle onto the couch with a book.

"My dad was here," Chris said. "And his older kids stopped by for a few minutes, and my uncle Joe was here, and Aunt Karen, and their kids. And my grandma, but I see her all the time.

"Aunt Karen made the beans," he added. "Grandma made the pies. My mom can't cook."

70

"I made the turkey," Mrs. Brashares called.

Chris nodded. "This is the best we eat all year."

Chris and I played backgammon by the fireplace. After a while I realized how late it was, and got up to go home. "Thanks a lot," I said to Mrs. Brashares. "And you don't mind—about church?"

"Of course not, honey," she said. As I put on my coat and shoes she said, "Your parents coming to get you?"

I shook my head. "I rode my bike."

"But it's dark out." She got up. "I'll take you home."

"No, that's okay—it's not far. It was dark already when I came here."

"It wouldn't be safe," she insisted. "The streets around here are too busy. Chris, put her bike in the back."

When we pulled up into my driveway, I felt embarrassed by my house. Not because it was bigger or fancier than Chris's—though it was—but because it was so much colder and emptier.

Friday my parents both went into work, for an hour or two that stretched to four or five, because, they said, it was so nice to get work done without anyone interrupting. I watched TV and read a book and mooched around, wishing for something interesting to do. Saturday afternoon Mom got out the thirty-seven boxes that her Christmas Village came in, plunked them on the floor, and said, "Here. You

71

can set it up yourself this year." Then she and Dad went out. They debated getting a sitter for me. I kind of hoped they would. They usually hired this old woman from up the street, Mrs. Norris, and she always brought her crocheting and showed me how to make doilies. She reminded me of my nana.

"She's old enough to stay alone," Mom said. "She'll be insulted."

I wouldn't have been insulted.

Dad hesitated. "Want to have someone spend the night?" he asked.

"Who?"

"Your friends. That—that red-headed girl, she comes around a lot. Or someone else. Anyone you want."

"That red-headed girl hasn't been here since September," I said.

He sighed, as though I were being difficult. "Will you be okay on your own?"

"Sure," I said. "Aren't I always?"

"Well, keep the door locked, don't answer the phone if it rings, don't talk to anybody you don't know, and we'll be back in three hours."

"Whatever," I said. No way would they be back in three hours. It took forty-five minutes to drive to the restaurant, and they were meeting friends.

"Have fun putting up the Christmas Village," Mom said.

As if.

I had friends at my old school. I really did. The red-headed girl was Stacy, who'd been my friend since I was six years old. Who thought I was lying about what Brett did to me. Who had a crush on Brett, and was jealous that he talked to me at all. That day in the cafeteria she backed away from me like she thought I would go after her next. She didn't say a word, and afterward she didn't call me, and neither did anyone else. I thought someone would. After my first week at St. Catherine's I called her. I missed her, even if she'd been wrong about Brett, and I still wanted to be her friend, even if she didn't want to be mine. We'd been friends since first grade.

Her mother answered the phone. "Stacy's busy right now. She'll call you back," she said.

She didn't.

Now I looked around the shadowy living room. Thinking of Stacy made my stomach hurt. I really didn't like being alone. I thought about calling Jenna, but I was sure she was out having a good time, with her family or something. Jenna wouldn't be sitting at home.

I called Chris instead.

"He's not here," Mrs. Brashares said. "He's spending the night with his dad. I'm sorry."

"I thought—" I swallowed. Chris was supposed to go with me to church.

"We're going to pick him up on our way to Mass," Mrs. Brashares continued. "About quarter till eight, okay?"

73

"Yeah, sure."

"You doing okay, Abby?"

"Sure."

"We enjoyed having you over the other night."

"Okay." I hesitated. "Bye."

CHAPTER

12

I stayed up reading in bed until almost midnight, but my parents still hadn't come home. I thought about calling their cell phones, but figured I'd better not. Eventually I fell asleep. When my alarm clock went off at seven, I tiptoed into my parents' room. They were both in bed, sound asleep. I got dressed and made myself breakfast, and left a little note for them propped against the coffeemaker, where they would see it first thing.

Chris wasn't ready. Mrs. Brashares pulled into Chris's dad's driveway and honked, and sighed, and turned to me. "It's always the same," she said. She tapped the horn again. Chris stuck his head out the door for a second, mouthed something we couldn't understand, disappeared, then ran out a minute later tucking his shirttail in with one hand and clutching an untoasted Pop-Tart in the other. He slung his duffel bag into the front seat and threw himself into the back. "Breakfast of Champions," he said, holding up the Pop-Tart and laughing. When we got to church he had to run off and put on the altar server's uniform, which looked like a big white bathrobe with a rope belt. Chris's dirty tennis shoes stuck out the bottom. "I told him to wear his good shoes," Mrs. Brashares muttered. Chris had to sit on a bench near the altar; halfway through, he started swaying, half asleep. The other altar server, a girl I recognized from school, elbowed him hard, and he sputtered loudly when he jumped awake.

That was the most interesting part of the Mass. I felt disappointed; I'd assumed Sunday Mass would be livelier than school Mass. Father Micah's homily was longer and boring; I couldn't understand a word of it. We sang songs I didn't know. I tried really hard to find that moment of peace, but it wasn't there, not even in the singing-prayer part.

"You okay?" Mrs. Brashares asked.

"Mmm," I said. We stood in the entry room waiting for Chris to change out of his robe. Father Micah shook hands with a big line of people as they came out of the church. I noticed that most of the people looked happy. Maybe they felt holy. "Do you feel holy after you've been to church?" I asked.

Mrs. Brashares laughed. "I almost never feel holy, period," she said. "I usually feel more peaceful after I've been to church, though. Why?"

I shrugged, irritated. Somehow the church thing had let me down.

When I got home my parents were still sleeping. I threw my note into the trash, thumbed through the Sunday paper, then sat down in the living room and started to set up the Christmas Village I'd ignored the night before. An hour later my mom came downstairs. "Look how much you got done last night!" she said. "This looks great!"

"I didn't do it last night. I did it this morning. After church."

"I know you're having fun." She wrapped her bathrobe tighter around her waist and went to make coffee.

"I hate this Christmas Village," I muttered.

A few minutes later Mom came back. "Remember the year we bought the village?" she said. "You were, what, five years old? You were so excited, and you really wanted to set it up all by yourself. I always told you, when you were old enough, I'd let you." She smiled.

I remembered being five years old. I remembered buying the Christmas Village. I didn't remember saying I wanted to set it up myself. My favorite part about the Christmas Village was always setting it up *with* my mother, taking a whole afternoon, just her and me.

Back at school Mrs. Sumner started completely freaking out about the Christmas play. We still had a week left to rehearse, but we had to use part of that time to make the set—the backdrop and the furniture and stuff. St. Catherine's didn't have a stage, so we used the one at the Presbyterian church across the street. They were very generous about loaning it to us, Mrs. Sumner said, but not so generous, Chris said, that they'd let us make our set ahead of time.

All we really wanted was a backdrop that looked like a family room, with a fake window for one of the characters to look out of, and a fake fireplace for Santa to come down. We had a chair and a footstool and a horrible old fake Christmas tree. "We'll decorate it," Mrs. Sumner said. "It'll be beautiful."

"It looks like it's been chewed by a cow," Jenna said.

We didn't have a real cloth backdrop, just big sheets of white paper from the teacher supply room. We taped them together to make one giant sheet, and painted our family room and fireplace on that. It looked great. The problem was, it wouldn't stay up. We tried taping it to one of the existing backdrops, and then tying it, and then hauling all the backdrops into the flyspace and taping our scene to the back wall of the stage. Nothing worked. Finally I noticed some long thin pieces of wood backstage. We stapled the paper backdrop to them, then tied the wood to one of the backdrops. It worked!

"Hooray for Abby!" Chris cheered.

"Nobody," Mrs. Sumner said, "and I mean *nobody,* leans against that set. If it falls down again, I quit."

We wrapped a bunch of empty boxes in bright paper and added enormous bows. We strung lights and tinsel on the pathetic tree. People brought in more props—a newspaper holder, a lamp—and the set looked cozy. It looked fantastic. We'd rehearsed and rehearsed, and suddenly the performance was the next day.

"Oh, honey," Mom said that night, when I reminded her. "I'm so sorry. I've got a business meeting tomorrow night."

"But it's my play," I said.

"I know." She adjusted her glasses, swallowed. "And don't worry, I know you'll do just fine. Do you think one of your school friends can give you a ride home?"

"Can't Dad?" I asked.

He looked uncomfortable. "Well, the thing is . . . I'm going with your mother."

"But you said it was a business meeting!"

"It's the firm's Christmas dinner," said Mom. "We really can't miss it—not this year."

Of course they could. A Christmas dinner? Sounded like a party to me. I stabbed my pork chop with my fork. "You always say it's important for me to be more involved in things," I said.

"I do," Mom said. "And you are. It's wonderful!"

"But then why won't you come?"

"I wish I could," Mom said. "I really do. But I have to pay a lot of attention to my job right now."

"Is that Allister guy going to fire you if you skip the Christmas dinner?"

"Abigail!" said my father.

"He is not 'that Allister guy,'" my mother said. "He is the

senior partner in my firm. We accepted the invitation a long time ago, it's a catered dinner, and we can't back out."

"But it's important," I said. My parents didn't respond. "There's an afternoon show," I said, after a pause. "At one o'clock. It's for the school, but I guess you could come to that."

Mom and Dad looked at each other—a look I recognized and hated. It was when they were trying to figure out whose schedule was least important.

"I'm in court all day tomorrow," Dad said.

Mom sighed. "I've got clients scheduled for one o'clock. I'll try to move them, or I'll try to get to the end of your play. I know you're disappointed, Abigail—next time, let me know further ahead of time so we can plan, okay?"

Like it was my fault. Like I hadn't been telling them about my play for weeks. "Whatever."

"Don't use that tone with your mother," Dad said. "There's no call to be rude."

"Sorry," I said.

After a pause, Dad said, "Please don't pout. You can say all your lines for us tonight, in the living room."

"That's not remotely the same," I said.

"Watch your attitude," Dad said.

"Sorry," I said again, even though I wasn't.

CHAPTER
13

We were excused from our morning classes so we could rehearse one more time. Everyone was a little bit nervous. Chris, instead of getting jumpier, grew calmer in a way that I thought meant he was scared. "Are you kidding?" he said when I asked him. "I *love* this."

"I'm petrified," I said. I was, too. Not that it mattered so much. A petrified cookie, who could tell?

Chris looked me up and down. "You'll get used to it," he said.

"Used to being petrified?"

"No, dingbat. Used to performing."

Before the first show we did something I hadn't anticipated. Mrs. Sumner came backstage and called us all to gather in a circle. "Hold hands," she said, and everyone did so quickly that I knew most of them were expecting it. I was between Jenna and a girl named Sarah, who had a small part like mine. Sarah's hand was normal, but Jenna's was cold and damp.

"Dear most heavenly Father," Mrs. Sumner began. Oh, gosh, I thought. She's praying. "Bless this play to your work, bless these actors, and use them to your purpose. Our

Father, who art in Heaven . . ." Everyone joined in. After the Amen, Mrs. Sumner said, "Places, everyone. Stay quiet backstage. Jacob, you watch, and as soon as I'm finished with my introductory speech, start opening the curtain."

I stood still for a moment and added a quick prayer inside my head. *Dear God, please make my parents come.*

Chris said it was almost impossible to see anyone in the audience, unless they were sitting in the very front row. Our afternoon performance was for the lower school grades, so I knew that if my parents did come, they'd have to sit in the back. The first time I went onstage I looked right toward the back, and even though the last rows of people were in shadow I was sure I saw my mom. She must have canceled her clients! My heart leaped. I felt like a real Christmas Wish, all right. And I played my parts well—I didn't make a single mistake.

Chris and Jenna were really good. They even made the kindergartners laugh, which Mrs. Sumner had warned us not to expect because kindergartners almost never under-stood anything, much less thought it was funny.

After we took our bows Jenna was laughing from delight. "You were great!" I said.

"Thanks!" Her whole face glowed.

Chris walked by, looking less happy than before the show, which I thought was strange. "Great job," I said.

He waved the compliment off. "It was okay."

"Can your mom give me a ride home tonight?"

He made a face. "Sorry—Jacob's mom's bringing me home, after the cast party."

Jenna had overheard. "My mom can drive you," she said. "No problem."

I kept looking for my mom then, but couldn't find her. It didn't surprise me. I knew she'd have to go back to work. I went to after-care and fooled around with Chris and some other kids, and felt pretty happy. By the time Mom picked me up most of the other kids had left. I was helping one of the teachers stack the chairs upside down onto the snack table when she finally came.

"Hurry, hurry," she said. "You don't mind making yourself some cereal for dinner, do you? Your father and I have to leave in half an hour."

"I have to be back at the theater in forty-five minutes," I said.

For a second Mom looked blank. "Oh! Your play! I'm so sorry, Abigail. I don't know why I keep forgetting. Well, let's go through a drive-through, then, and get you something hot. Will it matter if I drop you off early? Do you think your teachers will be there?"

"Did you like it?" I asked.

Mom's face tightened. My first thought was that she'd hated it, thought I'd done a terrible job. Then I realized she hadn't come. "I'm sorry," she said. "I really wanted to be there. My meeting took longer than I'd hoped. I'll come to your next one, I promise."

My throat closed up so that I could hardly speak. "Okay."

She got me a cheeseburger and a Coke and some fries, and dropped me off on the steps of the Presbyterian church. No one else was there. The doors were locked. I sat in the dark on the cold stone steps and ate my soggy burger, and felt so alone it made my stomach clench. Then a car pulled up, and someone got out and waved to the driver, who honked and pulled away, and it was Chris.

"Hey," he said. He sat down beside me. "What's up?"

"Nothing."

"Why are you crying?"

"I'm not."

He didn't say anything. I blew my nose on the paper napkin. He tapped his feet on the steps.

"You nervous?" he asked.

"About the *play*?"

"Yes."

"No."

"You were this morning."

"Well, I'm not now."

"So what's the problem?"

I wadded up my trash and stuffed it into the fast-food bag. "You know what? The problem is that nobody listens to me. Not once. Not ever. *Nobody ever listens to me.*"

He turned and looked full at me. The light from one of the streetlamps slanted across his face. Everything about him was serious. "Here's the thing," he said. "I am listening. I asked why you were crying, and you wouldn't say. You wouldn't even admit that you *were* crying."

I took a deep breath, but before I could say anything a car door slammed in the parking lot. Mrs. Sumner came running toward us, smiling and saying, "Chris! Abby! Come on, let's go see if that set is still standing!"

CHAPTER
14

The whole time I was getting ready, putting on my cookie costume and rubbing glittery makeup around my eyes, I didn't want to do the play. While everyone whispered backstage and Mrs. Sumner told us a hundred times to be quiet, I didn't want to do the play. I didn't feel nervous or happy; when we prayed I didn't feel peaceful or holy. I didn't want to go home, but neither did I want to be onstage. I took my place in the wings. I could hear Mrs. Sumner in front of the curtain talking to the audience. Then she stepped down and took a seat, and Jacob carefully pulled the curtain open, and the play began.

I waited for my cue and I walked onstage, and something amazing happened. I *did* want to be there. I was happy to be there. I was a terrific Christmas Cookie, and later I was an even better Christmas Wish. It was like a miracle. *I love acting,* I realized.

Ⴍ

Sunday morning Mrs. Brashares picked me up for early Mass as usual. Also as usual, Chris was slumped half-asleep in the front seat. I fiddled a little with my seat belt. "I've decided," I said. My voice came out a little too loud, and I paused before finishing, "I really am going to become Catholic. At Easter."

Chris sat up a little but didn't say anything. Mrs. Brashares looked at me in the rearview mirror. "Are you baptized?" she asked.

"I doubt it."

"She needs a sponsor," Chris said to his mother. "I told her you could."

Mrs. Brashares nodded. "I will," she said.

Just like that.

I held off telling my parents until dinner Wednesday night. The becoming-Catholic classes didn't start until 7:30, so I couldn't get out of our Family Night meal. "Got much homework?" my dad asked me.

I'd put it off and put it off, but Mrs. Brashares was coming in about twenty minutes, so I had to say something. "No, but I've got a meeting at school. My friend's mom is picking me up."

"What time will you be home?"

"I don't know. Couple hours."

We ate in silence for a few minutes before my mom asked, "What's the meeting about?"

"Becoming a Catholic," I said.

Somehow the silence after I said that was louder than

the silence beforehand. After a long pause, my father cleared his throat and said, "Don't be silly. You don't have to be a Catholic. Don't let them make you think so."

"They aren't," I said. "It's my idea. I want to."

Dad looked angry, much more so than I expected. Making him angry was part of my plan, of course—but maybe not this angry.

"Why?" Mom asked.

"I like going to church. Plus I want to believe in something."

Dad burst out, "You can believe in something without it being Catholicism, can't you? How about Wicca, have you thought of that? Or Kabbalah, that funky Jewish stuff Madonna's into?" I'd never heard him so sarcastic. "Catholic! Next thing you'll be telling me you've turned Republican!" His face was practically purple.

My mouth hung open. I could hardly breathe.

"Edward!" my mother said. "We'll discuss this later."

Dad pointed his finger at me. "You're not going to be Catholic."

I said, "You can't stop me. Father Micah says I'm old enough to choose for myself."

"Oh, I can stop you," he said. "Go to your room. Now."

I went. A few minutes later I heard Mrs. Brashares pull into the driveway. I crept very quietly down the stairs.

Dad was talking to her at the door. His face was back to a normal color, but he was using his angry trial lawyer voice.

"I don't understand how this could happen," he said. "I told that priest from the beginning that I didn't want him converting my daughter. I don't appreciate you or anyone else brainwashing Abigail."

Mrs. Brashares didn't budge. "Anti-Catholicism," she said, with an upward flick of her eyes at me, coming down the stairs, "is the last socially acceptable prejudice in this country."

"I am not prejudiced," my father spat. "My daughter is not joining a church. She is not going anywhere. Good night." He shut the door very firmly in Mrs. Brashares's face, and he sent me back up to my room.

I undressed, turned out my light, and climbed into bed. Wicca? Kabbalah?

Here's the sick part. I really wanted my parents to approve of me. Not just about religion, but about everything. I wanted them to look at me with wide-open eyes, and smile, and say, "Why, Abby, what a good person you are! We should have listened to you about that boy—we know it wasn't your fault! We're sorry. We'll make sure nothing like that ever happens to you again." Then they would draw me into a big rosy family hug and keep me safe and nothing bad would ever happen again.

I wanted that so much. I felt like I could give up anything if I could have that. Being onstage, Catholicism, anything.

But even if I gave up everything, my parents still wouldn't be that way. It filled my heart with despair.

I wasn't going to budge, not one inch.

⚜

On Thursday morning when I came down to breakfast, my dad looked at me and said, "March upstairs and take off that uniform. We're sending you back to public school."

I stared at him openmouthed. Mom stared at him openmouthed. She looked as stunned as I felt. I guess he'd forgotten I'd been expelled from public school. I guess he'd forgotten I couldn't go back.

"Sit down," my mother commanded. I sat. She shoved a bowl of breakfast cereal under my nose, and I started to eat it. It was her cereal, not mine, and it didn't have milk on it, but I ate it and didn't say anything.

"You'll go to school today as always," she said. "*When your father and I have discussed this*"—she glared at him—"then we'll let you know what we decide."

CHAPTER
15

Here's what they decided: that there are religions worse than Catholicism. Because the other options for middle school in my town—aside from the ever-attractive homeschooling—turned out to be two fundamentalist Baptist schools that my Dad visited and said were even farther off the deep end of the Jesus scale.

Here's what I like about Jesus. When some people wanted to stone a woman to death, because she had done a terrible thing, he sat down on the ground in front of her and drew in the dirt. Hum-de-dum-dum. The crowd waited for him to say that she'd have to be killed, because that was the legal punishment for what she'd done. They waited and waited, and he ignored them all, drawing in the dirt, until I imagine they almost couldn't stand it. Then he looked up and said, "Let the person among you without sin be the first to cast a stone."

He went back to drawing in the dirt. After a while, he looked up again, and everyone but the woman was gone.

I wish I knew what he'd been drawing. Was it something mundane, like stick figures or a landscape? Or was Jesus an arty kind of guy? Did he go for a more Impressionist style?

Here are the world rankings according to my father: smart people, who maybe believe in God a little but don't let it get to them; pagans, Wiccans, and Madonna (the rock star, not the mother of Christ); most members of the animal kingdom; earthworms and your more intelligent insects; Catholics; one-celled amoebas; fundamentalist Christians; germs. I suppose your basic Presbyterians must be in there somewhere, and also Jewish people and Buddhists, but I didn't know whether they were higher or lower than animals on his religion scale.

So I asked him.

Predictably, he refused to answer. "What a ridiculous question," he said.

"Why don't you like God?"

"I do like God. I have nothing against God."

"Why don't you like people who believe in God?"

"I'm sure I like some of them," he said testily.

"Why don't you like Catholics?"

"They're so closed-minded," he said.

"Like you?"

He looked up at me sharply, but not angrily. My father was a lawyer through and through; he always appreciated a decent argument.

"You don't really know anything about them, do you?" I asked.

He considered before he answered. "I know what I read in the papers."

"And you think newspapers always tell the truth?"

"Of course not," he said. "But some of what I know is clearly factual. Catholics don't allow women to be priests, did you know that?"

I shrugged. "I don't want to be a priest."

"And . . . some of the priests . . . I don't know if you've heard about this, Abigail, but it was in the press a lot at one time, and this is factual, not opinion. There were some cases where priests did things to children that were a whole lot worse than what that boy did to you."

Wow. *What that boy did to you.* It was the first time either of my parents had referred directly to the reason I stabbed Brett McAvery, let alone admitted that Brett did anything. I swallowed hard, then looked at my father and realized he was expecting me to respond to the Catholic part, not the Brett part. I didn't know what to say. I thought of how my parents were afraid Chris would be trouble like Brett, but how the two were nowhere near the same. "I don't think the whole church is anything like that," I said at last. "I feel safe there."

"Good," my father said. "But it worries me that you've obviously been talking to this priest without telling us."

"I didn't want to tell you until I'd made up my mind."

He picked up a newspaper and flicked it open like he wanted the conversation to end. "You may have made up your mind, but so have I, and I'm your father. End of story."

I waited, looking at him until he looked back at me. Then I asked, "Am I baptized?"

"No." My mother, who'd come into the room halfway through our conversation, answered. "You're not."

"Why not?"

My father heaved a dramatic sigh. My mother said, "Why would we, honey? It's not important to us. Plus, we decided it was wrong to impose any kind of religious beliefs on you. We wanted you to be able to grow up and choose for yourself."

As soon as she said that, her mouth dropped open just a little bit. A-ha. The opening I needed.

"Good," I said, "because now I'm grown-up enough, and this is my choice."

It was the end of the argument, and we all knew it. Logic was the only god my father ever worshipped.

And if I had any doubts about my plan to become Catholic—any little worries over the fact that I didn't believe in God—well, they pretty much faded away. Because the plan worked: Right then, I had my father's full attention. For the first time in years, he may have actually listened to me.

❦

Drama wasn't much now, with the Christmas play over. Mrs. Sumner had us reading possibilities for the spring play. The spring play was always a bigger deal than the Christmas play, and she was struggling to find a good script that had enough parts and didn't require music or singing or cost too much money. I didn't realize it cost money to put on a play.

Everyone had useless suggestions. "We could do, like, *Lord of the Rings,*" said Joshua.

"Yeah! We could make wizard costumes, and big feet for the Hobbits . . ."

Before they got carried away, Mrs. Sumner said, "There's no script for that—"

"We could write a script," said Dominic.

"We aren't allowed to write a script." Mrs. Sumner sounded peeved. "We can't take somebody else's book and turn it into a play. That's stealing."

"How about *Harry Potter*?" someone piped up from the back row, but Mrs. Sumner glared her down so quickly that I wasn't even sure who it was.

"No *Harry Potter*," she said. "We can't do anything that's copyrighted."

"What's 'copyrighted'?" Mary Hannah asked.

Chris groaned. "Everything interesting, from the sound of it."

"No, I mean, what's it mean?"

Mrs. Sumner waved her hands a little and explained. "Copyright means the story is protected by law. You can't use it without permission. If a story's old enough it might be in the public domain, and then we could use it, but we'd have to write a script ourselves, and that would be hard. Any script we buy, we have to pay money to use. That's called royalties."

There was a lot of muttering. Nobody had any good ideas. I asked how much we had to pay to put on the Christmas play, and Mrs. Sumner said a hundred and twenty dollars. I was horrified.

"How much to do something good?" Chris asked. Mrs. Sumner looked more annoyed than ever, but I laughed because it was so close to what I was thinking.

♪

After school I went to talk to Father Micah. I wasn't as afraid of him as I used to be. I told him I tried to go to Catholic class on Wednesday but my Dad threw a fit and wouldn't let me.

Father Micah looked sympathetic, but not especially surprised.

"Anyway, then my parents said I could be any religion I wanted to when I was old enough to decide, and I told them that Catholics think I'm old enough now. They don't want to believe that, but if it's true, then they know they have to let me. So can you tell them it's true?"

He pressed his fingertips together, listening to me, and smiled. "Absolutely. Have them come see me."

No way were they going to do that. "Isn't there a rule book or something you could photocopy?"

"There is," he said, "but ask them to come see me first."

"Can I have a copy for myself?"

"Of proof of the age of reason?"

"Of the rules. So I know how to be Catholic."

Father Micah laughed. "There are some very boring complicated theological rules called Canon Law," he said. "You don't need to bother with that. Then there are the precepts of the faith—what you need to believe in order to be Catholic. You'll learn about them in your classes. The rest of it isn't rules. It's just faith and common sense."

Common sense I probably had. But faith?

"Is there some way of knowing what people really believe?" I asked him.

He frowned a little and asked me to repeat the question. I did, and added, "I mean, if someone says they believe Jesus is God, how do you know if they're lying or not?"

"I don't," he said. "No one does. Except God, of course. In a way it doesn't matter what you say you believe. It only matters what you *do* believe. God sees our hearts and knows the truth. I can't do that."

As I left his office I thought, *Good, I can lie.* If the only person who could know the truth about what I believed was God, and I didn't believe in God, then nobody needed to know the truth. It was the best thing I'd heard all week.

CHAPTER
16

I was thinking hard enough about religion that I pestered Chris in after-care. Even though it was blustery cold, all us after-care kids had been sent to the playground, where we huddled in clumps or ran like crazy trying to keep warm.

"Hey," I said, swiping the soccer ball Chris was about to kick and tossing it to some fourth graders. "How do you know you believe in God?"

"Hey," he said. "I dunno. Ask my mother, not me. I don't know what to say about that kind of stuff."

"So you don't believe in God." Hooray! I thought.

"'Course I do."

"But you said—"

"I said I didn't know what to tell you. I didn't say I didn't believe."

"But God and Jesus being the same thing, that's hard. Because Jesus was a baby and all."

One of the fourth graders kicked the ball to Chris, and he kicked it back. "Yep."

"And that whole thing about Communion being the actual body and blood of Jesus?"

"Uh-huh," he said. "Weird."

"And you believe it?"

"Sure. Why not?"

Of course my dad refused to go talk to Father Micah. He looked so shocked by the idea that you would have thought I'd asked him to speak to the statue of Mary out in front of the chapel, and told him I thought the statue would answer. But Mom surprised me. "I don't have any appointments for lunch tomorrow," she said. "I'll see if he's free then."

I didn't see her at school the next day. I didn't find out what happened when she talked to Father Micah, or what she said to Dad. No one told me anything except that I could go to the Catholic classes if I wanted to.

"Why'd you change your mind?" I asked Dad.

"I haven't," he said, looking stiff. "But when I was your age I went through a phase where I thought Communism was a good idea. I figure you'll outgrow this soon."

On Wednesday Mrs. Brashares picked me up. She stayed in her car while I ran out to it, and she didn't say much on the way to church. I wondered if she thought I was as strange as my parents.

The Catholic class felt like the first day of school all over again. Most of the people in the common room were grown-ups, and of the handful of kids, most were older than me. A couple were really little, so little I wondered if they should be up this late. Everyone had been meeting for a few weeks already, so they knew each other, and stared at me.

First we prayed. Then most of the adults sat down, and the older kids went off to another room along with our sponsors. The little kids went somewhere else. Father Micah came to our room and spoke for a little while, then some other adult spoke. The topic was "a church community." We drew a banner depicting our idea of community. At the end we rejoined the adults and prayed again.

It wasn't what I expected. Lots of words, but no rules. Lots of questions, but no answers. No decoder rings or secret handshakes.

"Don't worry," Mrs. Brashares said, "it gets better."

At home I waited for Mom and Dad to ask me about it, but they didn't. I expected Chris to say something at school, but he didn't. I told Jenna all about it, and she nodded but didn't say much either.

Finally, on the way to church Sunday, as we were driving to pick Chris up at his dad's house, I told Mrs. Brashares I was surprised no one cared. "Are your parents giving you a hard time?" she asked.

"No," I said. "They're ignoring it." I'd rather they gave me a hard time, actually. I wanted to rattle them. I wanted their attention.

She smiled. "That's okay. Religion's a very personal thing.

I'm glad you feel called to the church, but I wouldn't like you less if you didn't."

Called. I imagined God as a very old man with a long white beard, dressed in a long white bathrobe, sitting behind a big desk on a fluffy white cloud in heaven. I imagined him leaning back in his leather chair, pulling a cell phone out of his bathrobe pocket, and punching in my number. *Brring.* "Hello. God? Yeah, sure, I'll come to church. Whatever."

If God called my dad, my dad would have his secretary answer and say he was in a meeting. My mom would purse her lips and dart anxious glances into Mr. Allister's office, and finally say she didn't see any openings in her schedule right now, but maybe she'd get back to him. My mom would hate to disappoint God, but she'd do it anyway. Work, you know. Partnerships and all that.

CHAPTER
17

This thing about God on a cell phone stuck with me. On the day before Christmas break, I asked Rachel at lunch, "What would you do if God called you?"

She gave me a funny look. "He has."

"Really?" Rachel was not what you'd call an active participant at Mass.

"Yes, you dope. I'm Jewish."

"Oh." I thought about that for a minute, then laughed. So God was phoning Rachel, but Jesus wasn't. Then I said, "What do you think God's ring tone is?"

Jenna wrinkled her nose. "Something churchy," she said.

"No," said Rachel, "I bet not. How about—what's that song? 'What a Wonderful World.' You know—" She started singing.

"Nah," said Jenna. "Maybe not church music, but I bet there'd at least be violins."

Before elective period we had a class party, and then we had another party at drama, which got pretty rowdy since Mrs. Sumner didn't even try to keep order. I asked Chris what he thought God's ring tone would be. "'We Will

Rock You,'" Chris guessed, and then he went around the room playing an air guitar and chanting, "We will, we will rock you. UNH. Rock you. UNH," so he was completely useless for the rest of the hour. I wanted to tell him Merry Christmas, but I didn't get the chance.

They didn't have after-care because of vacation, so I walked out the main door with the entire drama class. We were all wearing the Santa hats Mrs. Sumner had given us, and I was laughing and feeling really excited about Christmas, even though my parents had decided at the last minute that they really couldn't spare the time to visit my cousins after all. "Maybe next summer," Mom had said.

Then nobody came to pick me up. Chris left; Jenna left; everybody left until out of the whole class it was just Mrs. Sumner and me standing on the curb in the cold wind looking at the empty parking lot. Then out of the whole *school* it was just Mrs. Sumner and me.

Mrs. Sumner gave me her cell phone to call Mom's cell phone. Mom didn't answer. I called her office, and spoke to her receptionist. "She's in a meeting," the receptionist said. "Is it an emergency?"

I didn't know if I qualified as an emergency. I hung up and tried Dad. He answered. "I have to pick you up *now*?" he said. "Look, Abigail, I've got a meeting in fifteen minutes—"

"Mom's in a meeting—"

"Well, she'll just have to—" He bit that off. "Can't one of the teachers run you home?"

103

"I don't think so," I said. "I don't have a house key."

Now my father made an exasperated sound. Mrs. Sumner looked at her watch, and I felt like crying. "I'm sorry," I said.

"Don't worry," Dad said. "Somebody will pick you up right away."

He sent his secretary. She took nearly half an hour to get to school, and she looked really annoyed about running personal errands for my dad. Even Mrs. Sumner looked annoyed. "I'm sorry," I said again.

"For heaven's sakes, Abby, it isn't your fault," she said. "Didn't your parents read the school calendar?"

❦

I sat in Dad's office lobby for three hours. I didn't have any homework, of course, because not even the nastiest teacher would give homework over Christmas break, and I didn't have a book to read, and the only magazines in the waiting room were incredibly boring legal ones. When Dad finally came out the door, his receptionist said, "Mr. Lorenzo, your daughter is the quietest girl I ever saw." Dad gave a little jump. I swear he'd forgotten I was even there.

At home my parents had a great big fight about whose fault it was. It started out with who didn't read the calendar, who never read the calendar or paid attention to the house, and then it turned into whose job was more important. Then they got quiet and I thought they'd simmered down, so I went through the family room just to get a book, and my father looked at me and said, "None of this would be an issue, Abigail, if you hadn't gotten into trouble in school."

I wanted to belong to any family but my own. I almost kept quiet, but I took an enormous breath to steady myself and suddenly screamed back, "I wouldn't have gotten in trouble if you paid any attention to me! If you ever listened to anything I ever said at *all*!"

I ran upstairs and slammed my door shut and locked it, and then I did the strangest thing. I climbed into bed, under all the covers, and I went right to sleep. I vaguely heard my parents shouting, and later someone pounding on my door, but I didn't pay attention. I was that tired.

When I woke up, it was the middle of the night. Moonlight streamed into my window. My bedroom door stood open—they must have found the key. I wondered why they didn't wake me. I was hungry, but I didn't get out of bed. I lay and stared at the patterns on the ceiling. I knew that what I yelled was absolutely true. I also knew that it wasn't the complete truth.

☙

The next morning my parents were pretty quiet. In keeping with family tradition, we ignored the fight from the night before as well as my outburst. Mom made my favorite pancakes for breakfast and Dad poured me orange juice and asked if I'd like him to take me shopping in the afternoon. We went shopping. I bought him and Mom Christmas presents. It wasn't a bad day, and I knew my parents were trying hard to be nice to me, but I felt distant from them both, as though somebody'd stuck a big piece of glass between us. I couldn't really touch them, and I didn't care to try.

On Sunday morning Mom slept in. Dad jogged, and I rode my bike to church.

On a bike it was a long way, longer than I thought it would be. The cold wind made my eyes water. I pedaled as hard as I could, but still got to church late, and I was so cold that when the warm air from the church hit me I gasped with relief. Father Micah had already lighted the fourth Advent candle, and everyone was standing to sing the Gloria. I slid into the pew where I usually sat with Mrs. Brashares, and sang along.

By the time we'd gotten to the first reading I wasn't sure why I'd bothered to come. Who was I kidding—my parents or myself? I didn't belong in a church. How could I believe in God? If God loved and took care of everyone, why would he have let Brett McAvery—

I snapped my mind shut on that thought. It didn't matter. Father Micah preached his homily about the Fourth Sunday of Advent but I didn't hear a word. I sat in the pew and tried not to dread the cold ride home.

When I finally got back, my parents were actually angry.

"You're late," Mom said. "You usually get back from church half an hour before this. What happened? If something special comes up, you need to call and let us know."

Okay, sometimes weeks could go by without my parents noticing me. Suddenly they're worked up about half an hour?

"I rode my bike," I said. "Chris and Mrs. Brashares went to Michigan."

They'd be gone the whole holiday, which stunk. "*They* don't hate their relatives," I said.

Mom and Dad exchanged glances. "We don't hate our relatives," Mom said. "It's just this one year. Just until I make partner. We'll go back to Cleveland next year. I didn't realize it meant so much to you."

I hadn't realized it meant so much to me either. Spending holidays with the relatives was just something we'd always done.

"What if you *don't* make partner this year?" I asked.

Mom looked startled, like she'd never considered the possibility. "I should," she said. "I've certainly billed enough hours." Then she looked right at me and said, "I don't know. I haven't thought about it. If I have to think about it later, I will."

That afternoon I went upstairs and lay down on my bed. I had no reason to be tired after sleeping so much the night before, but I still felt like I was living behind a piece of glass, and I thought I might as well sleep as do anything else.

Mom came in very quietly and sat on the edge of my bed. She started to speak three or four times before she actually got words out. I watched her from a long way away.

"I've been thinking about Christmas Day," she said at last. "What do you want to do?"

I didn't answer. She looked worried. She said, "I assume you want to go to church? Would you like me to go to church with you?"

I wished I could go with Mrs. Brashares. Or not go. Or something. I wished I could tell Mrs. Brashares that I hadn't found any peace at church this morning, not one speck, and ask her if she ever had days like that. I wished I could tell my cousin Debbie that the knife had both worked and not worked, been both good and terrible. I'd really looked forward to seeing Debbie at Christmas.

Mom kept watching me and I realized she was waiting for an answer. "Okay," I said at last.

"Good," she said. "I just thought—well . . . well, good. You'll tell me what time?" I nodded. She patted my shoulder a moment, and left.

CHAPTER
18

At the last minute on Christmas morning Dad decided to go to Mass too, though I couldn't imagine why. He sat stiff and uncomfortable all through the service. He wouldn't sing, not even the carols like "Joy to the World" that everyone knows. I made a big show of crossing myself with the holy water going into the church, and genuflecting when we got to the pew. I said all the responses loudly and I sat down and stood up fast, so that my parents were always caught off guard, so that they felt as out of place as I did on my first day at St. Catherine's. Probably this was not a Christian way to behave. Not being a Christian, I wouldn't know.

On the way home Dad didn't say a word. Mom said, "How nice. I haven't been to church on Christmas since I graduated from college."

"Oh," I said, "I thought you were always a heathen."

That struck me as hilarious.

We opened gifts after church, since my parents had decided that, to me, church must be more important than presents. Part of my brain recognized that they were trying to understand me. Part of me wondered why they didn't just ask which I wanted to do first.

Anyway, the first gift I opened was a Bible. It was leather-covered, and bigger than the one Father Micah had given me. The second was a book that made the Bible look small: a complete collection of the plays of William Shakespeare. "He's the greatest playwright that ever lived," my father said.

Okay. I knew they were trying. I could see it. But I still felt so far away.

My third gift was a plaid purse shaped like a little backpack. I sucked my breath in when I saw it, and my mother interpreted this to mean I was delighted.

"I remembered!" she said. "It's just like the one your friend Stacy has!"

Stacy'd gotten it when she was shopping for back-to-school, and it was true, I'd loved it, and my mom hadn't wanted to buy me one, but she must have gone back for it and saved it for a gift. It was a nice thought, except that I hated Stacy now and didn't want to be anything like her, and that included wearing her stupid purse.

"Thanks," I managed to say. "Thanks a lot."

The rest of the vacation dragged by in a fog of bad weather. I'd never been so happy for school to start again.

Q

On the very first day back, Mrs. Sumner told us she'd chosen the spring play. She passed the scripts around. It was based on a book, she said, and she told us the title but it wasn't anything I'd ever read. The main character was a girl named Ruthie who had six brothers and felt like no one understood her. She was a little girl—eight years old, according to the first page of the script—but she was bold and tough, and she fought to get her way.

I grew so absorbed in the script that I stopped listening to Mrs. Sumner. I liked Ruthie. She was funny, and she didn't let anybody push her around. If I'd been more like her, I thought, I wouldn't have gotten into so much trouble. I wouldn't have gotten kicked out of middle school, if I'd been brave like Ruthie. If I'd been tough enough right from the start.

After I'd read a few more pages I forgot about myself, because I became so engrossed in the story. One of the brothers, Paul, was Ruthie's buddy and had a pretty big part. Another, older brother, Joe, had to leave the family farm to go away to war—World War I, because the story happened a long time ago. He didn't want to go, but he tried so hard to be brave—and Ruthie was the only person who seemed to understand how awful it was for him. She was the only person who understood who Joe really was.

As I turned the next page of the script, I looked up and caught Chris's eye. I smiled. Right then I knew exactly what I wanted to happen. I wanted to play Ruthie, and Chris to play Joe.

"The best parts are for girls," Chris complained at after-care. "Ruthie has twice as many lines as anybody, and Mother's got a ton too, and those twins."

"You have to be Joe," I said. "You have to."

"I think the Paul part is bigger."

"The Joe part's better."

"Probably." He shrugged.

"I want to be Ruthie," I said. I waited for his reaction.

He thought, then nodded his head. I grinned. Chris might blow off my religion questions, but he took drama too seriously to fool around. "You better *nail* your audition," he said. "Make sure you pick a long piece, to prove you can memorize a lot. Aren't you glad you were good at being a stupid Christmas Cookie?"

CHAPTER
19

There hadn't been any Catholic classes over Christmas break. I was a little surprised by how much I missed them. Nothing much ever seemed to happen in them, but I guess I liked going.

The first Wednesday after school began again, when we got to the church, a whole bunch of people were crowded around this old man, Mr. Spanish. I usually avoided him, because he looked so creepy—half-starved, with sunken cheeks and droopy flesh hanging off his arms. His skin was yellow gray, and had this really strange look to it, like it was made out of wax. He hardly ever said anything, but when he did his voice creaked like his vocal cords had rusted shut from disuse. And he never seemed nice, or sweet like somebody's grandpa. Mostly he seemed cranky. He was the kind of old man who made little kids cry.

All the adults at Catholic class were nice to him anyway, which was something I liked about Catholic class. They were nice to me too, even though I never talked unless I had to.

When we saw the group around Mr. Spanish, Mrs. Brashares said, "Oh, no," and hurried toward him. I didn't want to follow, but Chris grabbed my arm and made me.

Mr. Spanish sat very erect in his chair, his head high. A few of the women had put their hands on his arms or shoulders, but he acted like he didn't notice. Someone said, "Are you sure?"

"Absolutely," he said, in his creaky, rusty voice. A few heads bowed.

I figured Mr. Spanish had decided to leave. Some people had quit coming to classes. Usually nobody made a big deal out of it, so I was surprised by how sad all the other adults seemed.

Mrs. Brashares touched Mr. Spanish's knee with her hand, very gently, then tapped me on the shoulder and walked to the kids' side of the room. I followed her. She had tears in her eyes.

"He's quitting?" I said.

She nodded.

"I didn't think it was that big of a deal," I said. "I thought everybody was allowed to quit."

Mrs. Brashares's eyes widened, and then she let out a small laugh. "Oh, Abby, he's quitting *chemotherapy*," she said.

"He has cancer?"

"Honey, why do you think he looks so sick?"

I looked over my shoulder. Father Micah was talking to Mr. Spanish, or praying with him—both their heads were bowed. "I thought he was just scary," I said.

Mrs. Brashares laughed again. "He can be both, you know," she said. "He can be both."

Because the spring play was a bigger deal than the Christmas play, and because, as Mrs. Sumner said, we were all experienced actors by now, for our spring audition we had to memorize monologues, which were just big long speeches one person said alone.

Mrs. Sumner had whole books of monologues and let us pick any we wanted. I took Chris's advice and chose a long one, one that sounded like Ruthie in my head. I practiced it and practiced it, every night after dinner.

Dad poked his head in my room one night. "What's all the shouting?"

"A monologue," I said. "Auditions for the spring play. I want to be Ruthie."

"Ah." He looked like he didn't know whether he should leave me alone or stick around for a while. "So . . . you really like drama, don't you?"

"Yes," I said. "I do."

"Good," he said. "I'm glad to see you . . . good." He nodded his head again. "Did you like that Shakespeare book?"

I'd glanced at it—the gilt pages crackled when you opened them. It was 1,260 pages long, counting the index, whereas my Christmas Bible, Today's Catholic Edition, was 1,393, actually longer despite the fact that the Shakespeare book was three times thicker. I'd read a few pages here and there, but not a word made sense to me. Verily, I sayeth, and all that.

My dad stood looking at me. With a start I realized he was waiting for an answer. "Um, it's pretty," I said. "There are poems at the end."

He smiled. "I'm glad you like it," he said.

He went back to the family room and I started my monologue over. I wanted to be able to say it as naturally as if I'd just started talking to a friend on the street, and to do that I had to have it memorized absolutely perfectly, so that every word and inflection could flow without a hitch. I had to move enough, but not too much, and keep both feet firmly on the ground and never, ever, cross my arms over my chest. I had to look and sound completely comfortable. I had to speak loud and slow. Slow was the hardest part. It was easy to talk too fast, especially when I was nervous. I practiced saying my speech twice as slowly as any normal person would talk, so that when I sped it up a little it would be just right, not rushed at all.

❦

I'd never wanted anything as much as the Ruthie role. Before my audition my hands were shaking and I could hardly breathe. But as soon as I stood up, in front of the class and Chris and Mrs. Sumner, I felt perfectly at ease. I felt like someone other than myself. I did nail that monologue—I said everything just the way I wanted, loud and clear, and I didn't rush or miss a word—and yet at the end I didn't think it was going to be good enough. Jenna was perfect, and some of the other girls were really good, and most of them were seventh or eighth graders, more experienced than me.

Mrs. Sumner didn't keep us in suspense long. The very next day, at the start of class, she made what I already recognized as her traditional speech about our parts, which basically was that we weren't allowed to whine to her if we didn't like what we got. No small parts, only small actors. Blah, blah. Then she passed out the cast list.

I was sitting right in the corner front row, so I was one of the first people to get a copy. I knew that at least half the girls in the class wanted to be Ruthie, so I didn't say anything when I saw my name, and I tried really hard not to laugh. There it was, at the very top:

Ruthie—Abby Lorenzo

I had to bite my lip, it was so hard not to giggle. So hard not to shout.

Jenna squeezed my arm. "Congratulations!" she said. I scanned the list for her name. She was Mother, a good part. Then I looked for Chris—and he was Joe! Perfect!

I rummaged in my backpack for a highlighter, opened my script, and started to mark my lines. Mrs. Sumner was repeating her speech about being grateful for the part you had to a couple of kids who didn't look the least bit grateful, but I only half listened. I was grateful. I was beyond grateful.

I was Ruthie.

Ruthie.

Me.

I did it! I did.

I kept highlighting the script. Half the first page was yellow. All my lines. I flipped the page and started again. Rachel leaned over Jenna's shoulder to see. "Ohmigosh, Abby, you've got so many lines!" she squealed.

This drew Mrs. Sumner's attention. She looked right at me. "It's a lot to memorize," she said.

I looked right back at her. "I'll learn it," I said.

She nodded, and turned her attention to someone else. I looked at Chris. He grinned and flashed a thumbs-up. I grinned back. We were going to be great.

☙

January was a good month. School went by quickly. I did my homework during after-care, and at night after dinner I worked on my lines. To my relief Mom and Dad didn't ask to go back to church, and they didn't hassle me about going. Catholic classes were fine. One week the kids' group stacked cans in the church food pantry, and I liked that.

Then the first week in February came, and with it Ash Wednesday, and trouble.

CHAPTER
20

Ash Wednesday, I had learned, was the first of the forty days of Lent, a time of repentance leading up to Easter. In school they said Lent lasted forty days because Jesus suffered forty days in the wilderness before he began to preach. Lent prepares us for Jesus' death.

"Not for his death," Mrs. Moffett corrected me in class. "For his resurrection. Everyone dies. Jesus conquers death."

Okay, got that. But I looked at the calendar on the cover of my school planner, and I started counting, and I noticed that Lent wasn't really forty days. It was forty-six.

I raised my hand.

Mrs. Moffett said not to be ridiculous. Lent was forty days.

But it wasn't. I pointed this out, showing her my calendar.

She set her lips into a thin line, and I could tell she was annoyed, but she looked at the calendar and counted to herself. I was right. Of course I was right; I could count to forty-six.

"Well," she said, "I'll ask Father Micah."

I thought this was terrible. She's been Catholic for how

long, and she never counted the days in Lent?

Someone raised her hand in the back and said, "The Sundays don't count, that's why. If you give up chocolate for Lent, you don't have to give it up on Sundays."

Jenna said, "That's not true!"

"Yes, it is!"

"When you give something up, you have to give it up for the whole time!"

I was confused. Everyone talked at once for a while, and then Mrs. Moffett got the class settled down, and I learned the following things:

1. You are supposed to give up things for Lent.

2. You do this so that you suffer the way Jesus suffered in the desert.

3. Therefore, giving up chocolate is good. Giving up asparagus is bad. Giving up doing your homework is worse.

4. If you're allergic to chocolate, you can give up ice cream or popcorn instead.

5. On Easter you can pig out, the way Jesus pigged out when he came down from the desert.

6. Theoretically you can decide to do good things during Lent—pray the rosary every day, Mrs. Moffett suggested—instead of giving up something you like, but no one in the class seemed to think that doing so got you quite as many brownie points from Jesus.

7. If you did pray the rosary every day of Lent, including Sundays, you would pray 2,530 Hail Marys before Easter.

☙

None of this was so bad. I mean, I could live with giving up chocolate. I liked chocolate a lot, so it'd be a good sacrifice. I kept that to myself, though. The whole point was to not make a big deal about it.

That night Mom made roast chicken for dinner. It took a long time to cook, so we were still eating when Mrs. Brashares came to pick me up for Catholic class. Chris came to the door and knocked, and I got up and went straight away. I was glad to see Chris. Sometimes he came to Catholic class and hung around the back of the room, but mostly he stayed home or went to see his dad.

He frowned as we got into the car. "What were you eating?" he asked.

"Chicken," I said. "Mmm, good."

"You can't eat chicken on Ash Wednesday!"

Oh. Right. I'd forgotten. They'd served cheese pizza for school lunch.

Another funky Lent rule: no meat on any Fridays, and no meat on Ash Wednesday. I guessed it was because Jesus didn't have meat on Fridays out in the desert, though I wasn't really sure, because when you think about it, he didn't have cheese pizza either.

I knew the no-meat rule, but I'd ignored it. In the first place, my Mom would have had a stroke if she went to the trouble of roasting a chicken and I didn't eat it. In the second place, I had to eat something—and the chicken was awfully good. And in the third, I didn't really believe in vegetarianism.

Give me credit, though. I could have told Chris I forgot. Instead I said, "Come on, Chris, it's not like the sixth commandment is Thou shalt not eat meat."

He looked even more annoyed. "It's important," he said. "You shouldn't laugh about it."

"It is not important!"

"It is too!"

"Not to me," I said. "It's not like I actually believe any of this God stuff."

I saw Mrs. Brashares glance up to look at us in the rearview mirror, but she didn't say anything. Chris, on the other hand, went nuts.

"What do you mean you don't believe in it? That's the stupidest thing I ever heard! Man! Are you kidding? You can't make a joke out of this!" He slammed his fist against the car seat. I jumped. I'd seen Chris lose his temper in school maybe three hundred times. But never at me.

"I'm not making a joke out of it," I said. "I just don't really believe in it."

"You *have* to believe in it!"

"No, you don't," I shot back. "All you have to do is go to class."

His eyes were dark black and his face turned crimson. "You do," he said.

"When I asked you why you believed things, you told me to ask your mom, you didn't know."

"I can't explain it," he said. "That doesn't mean I don't believe it."

"Well," I said, "I don't."

He was silent for a moment. He crossed his arms and looked out the window. Mrs. Brashares didn't say anything, either. Then Chris said, very quietly, "Why are you doing it, then?"

I was determined to be honest. "To make my parents mad."

He made a noise like he was spitting. Then he said, "You're really wasting my mom's time."

Wow. I'd never thought of that. I felt bad about it.

Nobody said anything the rest of the drive. When we got to the church Chris rushed ahead. I don't know where he went because he never showed up in the classroom the kids' group used, and he didn't come into the common room at the end when we were all praying together. Mrs. Brashares left for a little while, so I guessed she went to find him and make sure he was okay, but she didn't say anything to me about it, and I didn't really feel I had a right to ask. I thought of her coming to pick me up every single Wednesday evening, and every Sunday morning. Chris was right. I was wasting her time.

We'd had an Ash Wednesday Mass at school, and Father Micah had smeared his thumb in black ashes and wiped some on everyone's forehead. One of the teachers smeared Father Micah's forehead too. I'd washed my mark off when I got home from school, but here in class the people around me sat with the black marks still on their foreheads.

As Father Micah wiped the ash on my head he had said, "Remember, you are dust." And I'd said back, as Mrs. Moffett told us to, "Remember, we are redeemed."

It was, absolutely, very hard to feel redeemed.

Which was probably why I opened my mouth.

In Catholic class I tried to keep to my policy of attracting as little attention as possible. I answered questions just enough to not get picked on. I knew everyone's name, but hardly talked at all. Even in group activities I didn't take up much space.

This time Father Micah came into our class. He started to talk to us about suffering, about dying to our sins so that we could be risen with Christ on Easter, about preparing the way of the Lord. Blah, blah, blah. I blurted out, without even raising my hand, "But why would a good God let bad things happen? Why would he let bad people even *live*?"

My voice sounded far angrier than I thought I felt. My voice sounded like I cared, like I was actually mad at God, like I really believed in him.

Father Micah paused. The whole room paused. Everyone looked at me, then back at him. "That's a very difficult question," he said quietly. "It's one that people have struggled with for centuries.

"I think you can look at it two ways. First, we only see one part of our lives at a time. We can't see the whole picture. Sometimes what seems like a terrible thing is really a blessing in disguise."

I must have made a face at that, because he paused again, and smiled at me. "I once knew a woman," he said, "not a friend, not someone I knew well, but someone I met. She

125

had been a fantastically talented figure skater, and she threw her whole heart into her training. She did nothing else. It was 1960, an Olympic year, and the top three finishers at the national championships would make the Olympic team. Skating in the Olympics had been a dream of hers ever since she could remember, and she had been competing very well and was expected to finish in the top three.

"But she didn't. She fell at nationals and finished fourth.

"That was the year the airplane carrying the entire U.S. Olympic skating team crashed in the Alps. Everyone aboard died.

"So finishing fourth was a blessing, not a curse. It seemed like the end of her dreams, but it saved her life. She just didn't know it at the time."

"That is so dumb," I said. "I mean, I get it, but you can't say the people on the plane—the ones who *did* make the team—deserved to die. And what about evil people? What about Hitler? Somehow the Holocaust was actually good, we just haven't figured out how yet?"

A ripple of whispers went around the room. Mrs. Brashares sat behind me; I couldn't see her face.

Father Micah held up his hand. He looked gentle, not angry; full of understanding. "I said two parts," he said. "The first is that we might not be able to see the whole picture. The second is that evil is real. It's a real presence, at work in the world, but it's not from God. Only good comes from God."

126

"So," I pushed him, "when something bad happens, God just sits back and watches?"

"God suffers with us," he said. "Look at Jesus on the cross. He bears our pain."

"It'd be a lot more useful if he did something to fix it."

"We are made to have free choice," Father Micah said. "We choose between evil and good."

I didn't say anything else, but I wasn't satisfied. In fact, I was furious. No matter what I said, Father Micah had a nice tidy answer for it. It was all easy, this religion thing, if you wanted it to be.

And what choices had I made?

I mean, besides taking out my knife.

⚘

On the way home Chris wouldn't look at me. He wouldn't speak. I tried a few times to say something to him, but his silence was so big and strong, I couldn't break through it. Mrs. Brashares didn't say anything either. I figured I'd completely blown it with my little bursts of truth-telling. Mrs. Brashares wouldn't be back.

CHAPTER

22

I was wrong. She picked me up for Sunday Mass as usual. I'd gotten up and gotten dressed, but hadn't been sure whether I should wait for her, or get my bike out again. I remembered how long it had taken me to ride to church before, and I'd just opened the garage door and was wheeling my bike out when Mrs. Brashares pulled into the driveway. I put my bike away and climbed into the car.

"Did you think I wasn't coming?" she asked.

"Chris was right," I said. "It's not fair to you. I don't really believe in any of this stuff, so you're just wasting your time. You could be doing something interesting on Wednesday nights."

"How so?" she asked, which was not the response I was expecting.

I squirmed. "Sometimes the classes are boring."

"Sometimes," she said. "Not always. I usually learn something."

"Probably you could be doing something fun. With Chris."

"I suppose," she said. "I doubt I really would, though. I'd probably put on my pajamas about eight o'clock, the way I do every other night, and read a book and have a glass of wine." After a pause, she said, "You don't believe in God, but you were getting up to ride your bike to eight o'clock Mass?"

"It really is bugging my parents," I said. I watched the gray clouds through the windshield. They looked like blankets covering the sky. "My mom's upstairs pretending to be asleep, but she isn't, because she's annoyed I got up so early."

"You're doing it for attention," Mrs. Brashares said softly.

"I had to do something," I said. "Otherwise it was going to keep on being like I didn't exist."

"Yet you hardly do exist," she said.

A splatter of drizzle hit the windshield and she flipped the wipers on. Swish, swish. I felt my stomach tighten, my breath get short the way it had all last year.

"Chris talks about his friend Abby who's so good in drama she got the big part in this spring's play," she continued. "I sit behind you every Wednesday night and see a girl who's trying to fade into the wallpaper. Which are you really?"

"I don't know," I said. "Mostly it seems safer to be wallpaper."

"Do you know why?"

I nodded my head. I knew, but I wasn't going to tell her.

She didn't push it. She said, "If you want to go to church or to classes, I'm willing to take you. You're not wasting my time. I'm doing this for *my* faith, not yours."

We stopped at a red light, and she turned to look at me. "Do you understand that?"

"No."

"I mean, I agreed to be your sponsor because you asked me to, and because if someone asks me to do something like this, I feel like I'm supposed to do it."

I thought about this. "You mean you think God's asking you, not me."

"Pretty much. And then . . . I think you're trying to figure out who you are. That's a good thing. Until you know who you are, you aren't going to understand why you do anything. Also—I don't know exactly how to say this, but it's okay with me if you going to church shakes up your parents. Church isn't a bad thing. And sometimes parents need to be shaken up."

I thought about that. "Do you?"

"Sometimes."

I was starting to be glad Chris wasn't in the car. "I just don't believe all this Jesus stuff," I said. "You say God's calling you, but I don't believe that. I don't."

"That's okay," said Mrs. Brashares.

"I maybe believe in God a little," I said. "Maybe. I mean, somehow the earth had to happen, right, and the universe? And if you think about it . . . well, I mean—"

"Might as well call it God," said Mrs. Brashares. "I agree."

That's not really what I meant, but she continued, "Everyone gets confused because so often people say God the Father, and that makes God seem like a human. If you think of God as a sort of universal Santa Claus, well, it's pretty easy to not believe in that. I think God's harder to picture than that. More complicated. Harder to pin down. So if you believe something helped start the universe, it doesn't have to be a bearded old man sitting on a cloud for you to call it God. Whatever it is, you can call that God."

"Okay," I said. "But I'm telling the truth. I don't really believe in Jesus and all that other stuff."

"You believe in the historical Jesus, right?" she said. "That he existed as a person, that he's written about in some historical documents that have nothing to do with the Bible?"

"Not really, but okay," I said. "It's the God thing I don't get. The Jesus-as-God, and that stuff about the Communion bread becoming his actual body. I don't believe any of that."

"That's okay," she said.

"So I can't be Catholic, can I?" I knew there was a list somewhere, of what I had to believe to be Catholic. I knew too that I couldn't lie about what I believed. I could see that now. I couldn't even bring myself to lie to Mrs. Brashares. How could I lie to God—assuming there was God?

"I don't know if you'll be ready for the sacraments this Easter," she said. "You know the Profession of Faith?"

I didn't until she reminded me. It was a big prayer we recited in church every Mass. It started out, "We believe in God, the father almighty, creator of heaven and earth," but went on to add a lot of other stuff. "The communion of saints, forgiveness of sins, resurrection of the body, and life everlasting." That was the end. We recited it during Mass, in one long, bored ramble: *WebelieveinGod,thefatheralmighty, creatorofheavenandearth* . . . I nodded.

"At Easter they'll do it in question form," she said. "Father Micah will ask, 'Do you believe in Jesus, the only son of God?' and if you aren't ready to answer yes, to that and all the other questions, you shouldn't join the church."

This broke my heart. I didn't know why. I wanted to be in the Catholic club, I just didn't want to have to believe. I leaned my elbows against my knees and put my head in my hands.

"It doesn't matter," Mrs. Brashares said. "No one will think less of you for having questions. You can go to Mass and to classes for years if you want to, before you take the sacraments."

"Chris will think less of me," I said. "He's already angry."

"Chris will get over it," she said. "Plus, this isn't about Chris. It's not his barbeque."

I had to laugh, but she was serious. "He can *come* to your barbeque," she said. "I can come, your parents can come, but it's not ours. It's yours. You're the one putting it on." She pulled into the church parking lot. "You call the shots."

I realized we still hadn't picked up Chris. "He's going to church with his dad today," Mrs. Brashares said. "Later on."

I missed him. I was glad I got to talk with Mrs. Brashares in private, but at the same time I wished Chris could have heard some of the conversation, so he'd stop being angry and speak to me in school again. I sat through Mass very quietly. When it was time for the Profession of Faith, I kept my mouth shut. I was surprised to realize that I knew the prayer by heart, that I could say it in my head along with the rest of the people without looking at the missal. I'd been praying it all along, on Sundays and on Wednesdays. I knew the words. I'd just never paid attention to what they said.

On the way home Mrs. Brashares said, "This is more of a beginning than an end. Let yourself have questions, pay attention to how you feel, and you'll be all right."

"I can't do it," I said. "I might as well quit now." My dad would be so glad.

Mrs. Brashares asked, "Why did you sign up for drama?"

I was so startled by the change in topic, I just stared at her.

"Why drama?" she repeated. "When you got to choose an elective, why did you pick that one?"

I thought back to my first miserable day at St. Catherine's. Art, I'd said. Then, when I couldn't do art, drama. "Just random," I said. "I wanted art, but my parents told me to pick something else. They wanted something more academic."

"So you picked drama?"

"To make them mad. Because it wasn't academic."

"Uh-huh." Mrs. Brashares acted like she already knew this, like somehow I was proving her point. "But it turns out you're good at drama. Really good, from what I've heard. And you must be, to get the lead role."

"Yeah, but—"

"So maybe some part of you wanted to act all along? Some part of you knew you'd be good. Maybe when you chose drama it wasn't entirely about making your parents mad?"

"Maybe," I said. "I don't think so."

"Yeah, I don't know either," she said. "I'm just saying, it's possible."

I thought about this. "You're saying I'm called. By God."

"Everyone's called. What I'm saying is that it doesn't matter. You're here, and if you want to be here, for now, just be here. Don't worry about it. If you're not ready to be baptized at Easter, no one will care."

I will, I said, but only to myself.

CHAPTER

23

Mrs. Brashares must have said something to Chris, because at drama on Monday he came and sat beside me, smiling his usual friendly smile. "Pax?" he said, holding out his hand.

"I have no idea what you're talking about," I said.

He thumped me on the head, a friendly thump. "It means 'peace,'" he said. "It means I won't be mad at you for wasting my mom's time."

"She doesn't think I'm wasting it," I said.

"Yeah, so she tells me. I still think you are. But whatever. Mom says it's called a leap of faith for a reason."

Mrs. Sumner called the class to order, and we started working. We rehearsed different scenes every day, over and over. I was in every one.

According to our rehearsal schedule, we were supposed to be off book for the first half of the play by now. "Off book" means you don't need your script anymore, because you have your part memorized.

Half the class wasn't off book after page six. That was a big scene with lots of people speaking, and everyone got confused, because even if they knew their own lines they didn't know the scene well enough to know when to say them. I did. I had the whole scene memorized—everyone's lines, not just my own. Mrs. Sumner prompted different people three or four times, and then she swelled up until I thought her head would explode, and she said that if we all didn't have that scene word-perfect by tomorrow she was going to start yanking parts, or maybe she'd just cancel the whole thing.

I knew Mrs. Sumner well enough by now to know that she'd never cancel the play. She would yank parts, though, and everyone knew it. Tuesday's practice was a whole lot better.

"Abby?" she said. "The way you just walked onstage, that was Abby walking. You're not Abby. You're Ruthie. Remember it."

Ruthie was feisty. She stomped onstage, and when she stood she threw her head up, looking people in the eye and daring them to argue with her. When she felt sad, she drooped. Ruthie showed all her emotions.

Ruthie was never invisible.

❦

There was something important missing in the last scene between Chris and me. I could tell, but I couldn't figure out what it was. The classroom we used every day was so much smaller than a stage that it was hard to move correctly, especially in the crowded scenes. But the scene that was causing trouble was just Ruthie and Joe sitting at a kitchen

136

table. We both knew our lines. I tried to sound little, and scared, and indignant, the way I thought Ruthie should sound. Chris tried to sound older, and brave and scared both, the way Joe should sound. But we weren't getting it right, and I knew it.

After class one day I asked Mrs. Sumner for help. She wrinkled her forehead. "I don't know what you mean," she said. "You're doing fine."

"It's not right."

"It's fine. I'm really proud of you, Abby. You're working very hard."

Chris knew exactly what I meant, but he didn't know how to fix it either. "We've got to completely understand what the characters are feeling," he said.

"How?"

He shrugged. "Get in their heads. Go deep."

"How do we do that?"

"Beats me, sister."

CHAPTER
24

In Catholic class we learned about forgiveness of sins.

I didn't anticipate this part. I'd kind of slacked off on my Bible reading, what with all the Ruthie going on. I knew the order of the Mass well enough that I understood we always asked for forgiveness right at the start. Lord have mercy. Christ have mercy. Like that. Sometimes we sang it. We were supposed to think for a minute about all the things we'd messed up lately, and then we sang about how we were sorry. It was a nice start to the service, but it didn't seem like such a big deal.

Well. This was different. I'd known already that all of us, adults and kids both, who were taking Catholic classes were divided into baptized and unbaptized. If you'd been baptized once, you didn't ever have to do it again. The rest of us were supposed to get baptized on Easter Sunday, right during the Mass.

I knew that, and I was okay with it. Once at a normal Sunday Mass a little baby got baptized—it was dipped stark naked into the pool of holy water, and everyone sang alleluia. There were a lot of prayers, of course. I was quite sure I wouldn't have to be naked, and I wouldn't fit into the little pool, so I imagined Father Micah would just have us dab our hands in or something. Fine.

This was the thing: Baptism removed sin. I didn't know that.

Something else also removed sin, and it had half the catechumens—the baptized half—in a twist. It was called the Sacrament of Reconciliation, and they had to receive it before Easter.

Father Micah spent a long time talking about the Sacrament of Reconciliation. He said it sounded scary, but it really wasn't. He went on and on about the beauty of it, and the wonder, the glory, etc., but not too many people looked like they agreed. The Sacrament of Reconciliation is a hard sell.

What you did was, you went into a little room with Father Micah, and you told him every single thing you'd done wrong, and you said you were sorry. Then he forgave you. Of course it wasn't him forgiving you, it was God forgiving you—not that it mattered much if you didn't believe in God.

I wouldn't have to do it, though. I wasn't baptized. Assuming I went through with this—and, since Mrs. Brashares hadn't said anything about my doubts to anyone, *they* were all assuming I would—the moment that holy water hit me all my sins got forgiven, presto, whether I admitted them to anyone or not, whether I was sorry or not.

Whether I was sorry or not. I didn't even have to be sorry.

I'd finally found the Catholic magic wand. Bing! You're forgiven!

Except that I hadn't gotten there yet. I hadn't gotten to the point where I could believe. I whispered to Mrs. Brashares, "What if you've done something unforgivable?"

She said, offhand, not whispering, "Nothing's unforgivable."

I knew that wasn't true. It couldn't be. I didn't believe in forgiveness any more than I believed in Jesus. I thought back to what I did in that lunchroom, to Brett McAvery with blood pouring down his arm, and I started to shake.

Mrs. Brashares grabbed my arm. "Abby! It's okay. Whatever it is, it's okay."

I couldn't answer. Now I was crying, and of course the entire room stared. Sometimes the children and adults' groups were separated, but not now. I felt my face burn red. I couldn't stop crying.

Mrs. Brashares put her arms around me and rocked me back and forth. "Shh, shh," she said, as if I were a baby. "Shh. You're okay. Abby. *Abby*. What's this all about?"

Creepy Mr. Spanish sat beside me. He'd gotten so weak, he had to use a walker, and I wished I felt sorry for him, but mostly he just creeped me out. He leaned forward and said, "I gotta admit, I don't believe it either."

Mrs. Brashares said, more fiercely than ever, "Nothing's unforgivable. Do you hear me? *Nothing.*"

"I been in a war," he said.

"Me too," I whispered. "Me too."

Tears streamed down my face. I wished I could crawl right into Mrs. Brashares's lap. I wished my mother ever held me like this.

Mrs. Brashares's arms tightened around me. "Nothing," she said again, more softly.

"Honey," Mr. Spanish said. *"Abby."*

I opened my eyes. He was leaning over, his face very close to mine. "What could a sweet little girl like you ever do that could be unforgivable?"

He looked straight into my eyes. I looked straight into his. All at once—and this is hard to describe—I could see that he was somebody's dad and somebody's grandpa, and that even though he was old and creepy and ugly, there were probably people who loved him. All of a sudden I thought, if God has a face, it probably looks like Mr. Spanish.

He took a deep breath and eased himself upright. "Well," he said, in a louder voice. "If it's true we can be forgiven, I can't wait."

I settled down, but I didn't believe Mrs. Brashares. No way. Twice a week at Mass I dipped my fingers into the same holy water they used for baptisms. Now, suddenly, it was going to be different? This time when I touched the water I'd be healed? I could just imagine what my father would say. It was voodoo.

"It's not voodoo," Mrs. Brashares said patiently, when I said this on the drive home. "It's not. You'll see."

"Huh." After a pause I asked, "What do you think the ring tone on God's cell phone is?"

"Mmm, good question." She thought for a moment and said, "How about 'R-E-S-P-E-C-T'? That old Aretha Franklin song. That would be a good one. What do you think?"

Rehearsals were still messy, but now that we all knew our lines Mrs. Sumner wasn't too frazzled. Yet. Part of the problem was that we didn't have enough room to move in our classroom. We didn't have any props either. But almost everybody knew their lines almost all the time. "The acting starts now," Mrs. Sumner announced on Monday.

We stared. I personally thought I'd been acting all along.

"Wednesday begins dress rehearsals," she said. "I've gotten you out of your afternoon classes for Wednesday and Thursday, and I expect you to stay at the school until six." Half the class groaned. Not like they didn't know this already. I glared at a few of the groaners. What, they wanted to do this without enough rehearsal? I'd rather work. Mrs. Sumner pretended not to hear. "Friday you're out of your classes all day. Performances at nine thirty, one o'clock, and six thirty at night. Got it?"

We worked hard, and I thought the class went okay, but at the end of it Mrs. Sumner pulled Chris and me aside. "This scene between the two of you," she said.

"It's not working," Chris said.

"Not entirely," she answered.

It was the scene I'd been worried about; the scene where Joe was going off to war. Ruthie says she knows Joe is afraid, and Joe says he's not, only he has to say it in a way that makes everyone understand he really is afraid. He talks about how much he loves the farm where they live. Ruthie begs him not to go, and he says, "I haven't got a choice."

It doesn't sound like much, but it's the most important part of the play, the heart of it. I knew this. "You were right," Mrs. Sumner said. "There's a little bit missing. It's hard here in the classroom. When we get onstage, remember that this scene has to work. If it does, the whole play makes sense. If not . . ." She looked hard at us. "I know you're friends, and I know friends sometimes have issues. If you do, drop them. I didn't cast you in these roles because you get along. I cast you because you're actors. Get it done."

We nodded. I wanted to explain that we didn't have issues, that my faith was not Chris's barbeque. But it was all too complicated. Some days I thought my head would spin off. Chris and I picked up our backpacks and walked out the door. We went over to after-care in silence.

☙

On Tuesday my dad suggested that for Family Night we all eat at a good Italian restaurant a half-hour's drive away. "We'll get you home in time for your religion class," he said, which was the nicest he'd ever been about it.

144

"I can't," I said. "I've got dress rehearsal until at least six, and I'm guessing it'll run over."

"Stay until five thirty, and leave then," Dad said.

"I can't."

He looked a little irritated. "Of course you can. Staying two and a half hours after school is late enough."

"Dad, I really can't."

My mom was a big fan of the Italian restaurant too. She said, "If you're worried about how it'll affect your grades, I'll have a talk with your teacher."

"I'm worried about how it'll affect my life," I said. "If I try to tell Mrs. Sumner I'm skipping out, she'll kill me."

My dad said, "Surely they can do without you for half an hour."

For a tiny moment I didn't answer, but then I said, very evenly, "They can't do a single scene without me. I'm in every one."

My parents didn't believe me.

"Every scene!" Mom said. "But you're playing the part of an eight-year-old!"

"I am. In this play that's the lead."

Dad said, "But on Wednesdays we always—"

"No." I felt something different inside me—a piece of Ruthie, maybe? I didn't feel angry, but I didn't feel like wallpaper either. I didn't feel like a girl Brett McAvery could scare and take advantage of. "*Listen.* This is really important to me. I can't skip it, and if I could, I wouldn't. Not the play. Not the

classes. You need to understand. I'm not skipping either one."
I looked right at Dad, and after a moment, he blinked.

"But you have to eat something," he said.

"I'll figure it out," I said. "I'll take a sandwich."

They looked at each other for a moment, and then they looked back at me. "Okay," Mom said. They didn't look angry. They looked like they were seeing me. The real me.

CHAPTER

26

Wednesday afternoon, rehearsal was a cosmic nightmare. I had expected it to be bad, but not this bad. There were sixteen separate scenes in the play. Some of them took place in front of the closed main curtain, and while that scene was going on, the set behind the curtain had to be changed to something else. There were scenes set at Ruthie's house, and scenes set at school. The ones in front of the curtain were mostly walking scenes—walking back and forth to town, or to school, or somewhere.

The curtain never shut when it was supposed to. One of us was supposed to shut it. (Not me; I was always onstage, or about to go onstage.) But no one ever shut the curtain. Then, after Mrs. Sumner bellowed, "Curtain!" someone would run to shut it, and you could hear the footsteps, and then it would shut on a chair that had been set too far out on the stage, and the chair would get dragged halfway across the stage, and everybody would laugh. Then Mrs. Sumner would bellow again, and we'd have to start the scene over.

Sometimes I was supposed to be carrying a doll, and I couldn't find it in the mess backstage. Twice I had to take my shoes off and put them back on, onstage. I was wearing laced ankle boots, because they were like the shoes Ruthie would have worn back then, and I couldn't get them laced in time. I had to play a whole scene wearing just one shoe.

Then we started forgetting lines. Everyone. Even me. There was a big scene set in the kitchen, and suddenly no one could remember what to say. I looked desperately at Chris, and he looked back and crossed his eyes. It was so unexpected, I started to giggle. Chris laughed. The people playing Mother and Father laughed, and Jacob, who was playing Paul, started to laugh, and Mrs. Sumner came down from the light booth and went absolutely flaming berserk.

She was mad enough to shock us into remembering our lines.

"Start over!" she screamed. She checked her watch, and I checked mine. Five twenty. The play lasted an hour, if we got the scene changes perfect, which we'd never come close to doing. After that we'd have to reset the stage and hang up our costumes, and then listen to Mrs. Sumner's notes. We wouldn't be done by 6:30. Not close.

On the other hand, if we didn't start figuring this out, we were doomed. At least I was. I didn't want the starring role in a disaster.

The curtain shut. Jenna was standing beside the rope that opens it, checking her script and scribbling notes on a piece of paper. She smiled at me.

"Places!" Mrs. Sumner screamed from the light booth. "Start!"

148

There was a mad rush as everyone found their places. I was offstage left, waiting in the wings with all the boys who played my brothers. Jenna pulled the curtain open. We paused one second, then all the boys rushed onstage, me following them.

"Give it back! Give it back!" I shouted. They had my rag doll, and they were playing keep-away. I rushed first one of them, and then the other, while they passed it back and forth just out of my reach.

Chris was wrong. You *could* see people in the back of the audience. I looked up, and right by the door, behind the last row of seats, stood my mother and father.

For a second, the tiniest second, I froze. Then I shook my head, and was Ruthie again.

Luther, the littlest brother, hurled the doll offstage. I whirled, and shrieked with rage. Chris came onstage, holding the doll, which was now dripping wet. (It was a second doll, a twin of the first, and we kept it in a coffee can full of water backstage.) Chris said his line: "Right into the pigpen." I shrieked again and clutched the wet doll to me. A small corner of my mind decided to let Mrs. Sumner handle my parents, if they needed handling, while the rest of me just kept acting. When I next looked up at the door, a few scenes later, my parents were gone.

149

At the end of the run-through we all sat on the edge of the stage, our legs dangling. Mrs. Sumner looked at us sorrowfully. "That was awful," she said.

We nodded. It *was* awful.

"Tomorrow will be better," she said. "The first day onstage is always hard. Go home, study your scripts, and sleep well."

I had Catholic class and a ton of homework. I walked out into the lobby wondering if I shouldn't just quit the Catholic stuff now. The lobby was filled with parents who had come to pick up their kids. Some of them looked irritated that we were so late, but most just looked resigned. My mom and dad were standing in one corner. They didn't really know any of the other parents, I realized, except Mrs. Brashares, and I doubted my dad would act friendly toward her.

When I reached them Mom smiled. Dad put his arm over my shoulders and handed me a big Styrofoam box. It smelled fantastic. Then I saw they had boxes too. Take-out from the Italian restaurant.

"Manicotti," said Mom. My favorite.

"Can we eat it here?" Dad asked.

Mrs. Sumner had told us thirty-seven times not to bring snacks or sodas into the theater. I shook my head.

"Well, we'll take you to St. Catherine's," Mom said. "We can sit in the cafeteria for a few minutes before your class, right?"

I guessed so. I looked over at Chris and he nodded, and I knew he'd tell his mom to meet me there. We walked across the street to the school. We took our dinners into the cafeteria and sat at one of the long tables. Part of the evening classes were held in the cafeteria, and some of the people who taught them were already rearranging tables and chairs and setting up a microphone. They smiled at me, but they didn't say anything. I opened my box. There was a plastic fork inside, and a little helping of salad and a piece of garlic bread next to the manicotti. I was starving.

My parents' silence began to seem odd. They were almost fidgety. Finally Mom spoke.

"I see why it's so important to you," she said.

Dad cleared his throat. "You looked different onstage. Not like yourself."

I grinned. "That's called acting," I said.

He nodded, his face serious. "I guess it is."

Mom said, "You didn't even notice us, did you? When we came in."

"I did," I said.

"Oh." She looked uncomfortable. She picked at her dinner and said, "You were right that we should have listened to you. We should have known about this before. What time is the performance Friday?"

"Six thirty."

Dad said, "We won't miss it."

I knew I was supposed to be grateful, and part of me was. But part of me thought I shouldn't have had to be the lead for them to care. Part of me thought they should have been

151

excited about my play even if I had a tiny little role.

Part of me was still angry that they hadn't been paying attention from the start.

Mrs. Hall, who was in charge of the kids' classes, came up and put her hands on my shoulders. "Are these your parents, Abby?" she asked.

I said yes and introduced them. Dad stood up to shake her hand.

"Did they come for the ceremony?" Mrs. Hall said.

Mom's eyebrows raised. Dad answered, "We came to bring Abby dinner after her play rehearsal, but if there's something to stay for, we'll stay."

"Wonderful," Mrs. Hall said. She smiled at me. "See you in a few minutes, Abby. In the church."

"What ceremony?" Mom asked after Mrs. Hall left.

"I have no idea," I said. "I didn't know about it. Probably just some prayer thing. We pray a lot. You don't have to stay."

"They aren't making you Catholic tonight, are they?" my dad said, laughing a little.

"No. That's next Saturday. At Easter Vigil."

From the look on his face, he didn't expect that answer.

"What happens on Easter Vigil?" Mom asked.

I'd learned so much in the last few months that it seemed almost incomprehensible that they didn't know. "I get baptized first," I said. "And then I get confirmed, and get to take Eucharist. It's a Mass, of course. Chris says there's lots of other stuff. Special stuff."

"Hm," said my dad. "And you're sure this is something you want to do?"

"Yes," I said. I bit my lip. Except for that not-believing part.

"You've certainly worked hard at it," my mom said. "We're happy to stay with you tonight."

"You don't need to. Mrs. Brashares will bring me home." I took a last bite of manicotti and stuffed my trash back into the box. "Thanks for bringing dinner."

"We'll stay," Dad said. "We'll take you home."

"It's okay," I said.

"We'd like to," Mom said.

"Really, it's okay."

"Don't you want us to?"

"Of course I don't want you to!" I said, more loudly. "This is not your barbeque! This is mine! My own, completely mine! I don't need you here. I don't want you here. I needed you last year, and I kept asking you for help, and you never would help me. Right now all I need is for you to leave me alone!" I crossed my arms on the table and buried my head in them. "Go away!"

It took a few minutes, but they went. One of them touched my head, but I shook the hand off. I heard them pick up their trash and walk away. I took a deep, shuddering breath, and went up to the church to see what the wretched ceremony was all about.

CHAPTER

27

Chris and Mrs. Brashares were waiting for me. "What's wrong?" Chris asked.

"Nothing." I slumped in a pew. "My parents are making me mad."

Mrs. Brashares sighed. "Wouldn't they stay? I'm sorry."

I didn't correct her. "What's this about?" I asked. Whatever it was, it looked almost ready to start. Most of the catechumens were sitting down.

Mrs. Brashares gave me a sympathetic look. "We'll pray first," she said. "And then everyone who plans to join the church at Easter will go up and sign the book of the elect. If you sign, it means you're committed to going ahead."

I looked at my hands. They were folded prayerfully, the way a good Christian's should be. "You could have warned me," I said.

"You don't have to sign," she said very gently. "You won't be the only person taking the classes who's not ready."

I got up. I walked past Mrs. Brashares, and I walked out of church. I made my way down the hallway into the school part of the building, and I kept walking, very quietly but fast. I was heading for the drama room, the safest place I knew. I heard footsteps behind me, and I thought it was Mrs. Brashares, but when I stopped in the classroom the person who followed me was Chris.

"What's up?" he said.

"I want to believe," I said. My voice shook. My hands felt shaky too. "I really do want to. I just don't."

"Oh," he said. He didn't look shocked, or angry. I sat on the rug near the front of the classroom, and he sat next to me, watching me, his face grave.

"Do you believe the earth's round?" he asked.

"Of course. Don't be an idiot. It's not the same."

"It looks flat," he said.

"I've seen those photos taken from space," I said. "All right? Not the same."

He thought for a minute. "If you were born blind," he said, "totally blind, you'd never understand about colors. You'd never really know what blue was, or yellow. How could you? But that wouldn't mean colors aren't real. They're still there, even if you can't see them."

I didn't say anything. One of his shoelaces was untied. I pointed at it, and he reached down and tied it. Looking at his shoe, he said, "Why'd you stab that kid?"

"What?"

"At your other school," he said. "You never talk about it, but it must have been a pretty big deal. What happened?"

I didn't say anything. Chris waited, watching me.

"What was his name?"

155

"Brett McAvery," I said. "He was like—all the grown-ups thought he was some kind of perfect kid, but he was really nasty. He was evil. Even in third grade he'd come up and whisper dirty words in the girls' ears, and he'd pinch us." I pulled my knees up and wrapped my arms around them. "In fifth grade he decided to pick on just me. He said a bunch of awful things, and I ignored him, and then he started asking why I didn't wear a bra"—it was hard to believe I was saying all this to Chris, but once I started, I couldn't stop—"so I started wearing one, and then he kept trying to snap my bra strap, so I wore a sports bra, and then if I wore a skirt he tried to pull it up, so I stopped wearing skirts, but he didn't quit bothering me, he just kept making it worse and worse.

"One day he caught me all alone in the hallway and was trying to pull up my shirt, and after that I tried not to walk anywhere alone, but I couldn't stay completely away from him—"

"Why didn't you tell anyone?" Chris whispered.

"I did! But it didn't change anything. My friends all thought he was really cool, and he was always nice to them, so they didn't believe me. And my fifth-grade teacher loved him, and hated me—I don't know why. And my parents . . . my mom says now that she didn't think a boy that young would act like that."

Chris snorted. I continued: "He wouldn't stop, and nobody would stop him, and then I got to middle school and he was still there. And right from the start he was worse,

156

and then it turned out his dad was the principal so I knew no one was ever going to believe me over him. So I bought a knife and showed it to him, and told him if he didn't stop he'd wish he had—"

"And he didn't stop," Chris said, very softly.

"And it got worse," I said. "He thought my knife was funny. And one day in the lunchroom he grabbed the back of my pants and said he was going to pull them down in front of everyone. And they were loose pants, they would have come down and I—I—"

"Stabbed him," said Chris.

"On the arm. The blade went a lot deeper than I thought it would."

"He deserved it," Chris said.

"See, I don't think so," I said. I'd thought about it a lot. Over and over, when I couldn't sleep at night. "I think he should have been punished, and I think he should have been stopped. I don't think he should have been stabbed. He had to go to the hospital in an ambulance. His parents wanted to sue my parents. Except a few kids said they'd heard him threaten me, so his parents dropped it. But my friends didn't say that—just some boys I didn't know."

"What happened to him?"

"I don't know."

"Do you care?"

I took a deep breath. "Yes and no. I never want to see him again."

We sat for a few minutes in silence. The room was all shadows, the only light coming from the hall through the open door. I kept expecting Mrs. Brashares to walk in.

"No wonder you think no one listens to you," Chris said.

"No one did," I answered. "No one." Until now.

Chris lay back on the rug with his knees pointing at the ceiling. "Look where we are."

"I love drama," I said.

He nodded. "It's family."

I realized all at once why I loved being onstage. It felt scary at first to be standing onstage with empty space and silence all around you, that you had to fill with your movements and voice. But really, it was the safest place in the world. There was only room for the character you were playing. There was no room at all for you.

No one came to find us. We sat for a while in the classroom, talking, and then we went quietly upstairs. Catholic class was over. It ended early, after the signing of the book of the elect. Mrs. Brashares was kneeling in the church; it looked like she was praying. Father Micah was messing with the sound system. One of the microphones squawked.

Chris nodded his head toward Father Micah. "Talk to him," he said. "He'll listen."

So I went up to Father Micah, and he smiled and led me into a little room like a closet off the main church. Mrs.

Brashares had showed me this room before. It was the forgiveness room. "I can't get any sacraments yet," I warned him. "I'm not baptized."

"Okay," he said. "What brings you here?"

I told him. I told him every last thing, about my old school and Brett McAvery and the people who wouldn't believe me, and my parents and Jesus and everything.

He listened. At the end he said, "Evil comes into the world where you least expect it."

I thought he meant me, what I had done. Tears welled out of my eyes, and I started to say, "I'm sorry—"

He laid a hand on my knee. "Not you."

I realized who he did mean. "Maybe he didn't know."

"Maybe. Maybe not. Still evil."

"But I was wrong too."

"Yes."

"I didn't think I had a choice."

"Did you?"

"I had lots of choices. I could have screamed really loud every time he came near me. I could have refused to go to school until someone paid attention to what I was saying. I could have slapped him, or pushed him, or done something else that wouldn't have really hurt him."

That was a lot of truth, right there. More than I wanted. I wished none of it had been my fault.

"When you pray," Father Micah said, "what happens?"

I thought of the prayers we recited in school, of how if

159

you rattled off fifty-five Hail Marys it was a rosary. I thought of the profession of faith that I couldn't quite bring myself to say. "Nothing," I said.

"Tell me about your prayers."

Which was when I realized that I wasn't really praying. I had been reading the Bible. I'd learned prayers. I'd recited prayers. I hadn't prayed. Praying would be talking to God.

"I don't pray," I said.

Father Micah leaned forward, his eyes shining softly. "You can't learn about God without spending time on your knees," he said, softly but very earnestly. "Knowledge and logic will only take you halfway there."

On the way home I asked Chris about prayer. "I don't really talk," he said. "I mean, I say thanks for the food. Sometimes I pray at night. But I don't say, 'Hey, God, I'd like to grow six inches taller and get a new Game Boy.' I figure God's got more going on. What does he care if I have a new Game Boy?"

"What do you care if you're short?" I was momentarily diverted. It was true I was an inch or two taller than Chris, but I didn't know that being short bothered him.

"I talk to God," Mrs. Brashares said. "Sometimes when I can get my whole mind to be quiet, and really talk to him, he answers, clear as can be."

Chris snorted. I said, "What does God say?"

She laughed. "Usually he tells me to get over myself," she said. "To quit wasting time worrying about stupid stuff. To trust. It's good; I always feel better afterwards."

"Did you talk to God about me?" I asked.

Her face went completely smooth for an instant. Then she smiled, like a little kid who's been caught doing something wrong but isn't really sorry. "Yes."

Chris laughed. "And?"

"God said you weren't my problem," Mrs. Brashares reported. "I'm not supposed to worry about you. Hey, how about this for God's ring tone? John Lennon—'Give Peace a Chance.'" She chuckled.

Chris groaned. "Never," he said, "give my mother a challenge."

☙

My parents were waiting up for me. They were usually awake when I got home from Catholic classes, but by then my dad would be messing around on the computer and my mom would be looking over her day planner figuring out what she'd have to do tomorrow. This time they were both sitting in the living room, beside each other on the sofa, waiting. My mother was drinking a cup of herbal tea.

"I made some for you too," she said, handing me a cup. I sipped it, and it was sweet—she'd put sugar in, just the way I liked it. It almost made me want to cry, which was ridiculous. What was sugar in my tea compared to Brett or to drama? I hated that she only paid attention to small things.

It occurred to me that someday I was going to have to forgive my parents.

Also myself.

Oh, this stunk. This religion game got harder the longer you played it. I did not believe in being forgiven, because I did not want to have to forgive.

I sat on the very edge of the couch, cradling my mug in my hands. "I'm really tired," I said.

"I'm sure you are," Dad said. "But your mother and I have something important to say. We didn't realize until today how much your religious studies mean to you, and how much you've wanted our support. We're sorry. We'll try to do better in the future."

"We can see that these are nice people you've surrounded yourself with," Mom said. "It's okay with us that you're doing it. Okay?"

For a second I didn't know what they were talking about, and then I realized they were responding to my outburst right before the start of class. "Okay," I said wearily. They still didn't get it. They thought what I'd said was all about religion and nothing about Brett. "Can I go now? I've got homework."

♇

I had so much to think about. It would be just super if I had any *time* to think. Now it was nine thirty and I had stacks of homework. I dragged myself upstairs, put on my pajamas, and sat down at my desk. My algebra was absolutely impossible. Algebra rarely made sense to me even when I was wide-awake. I shut the book, yawned, and went on to my reading assignment.

Fifteen minutes later I jerked awake. I'd drooled a big puddle onto the pages of my English book. I mopped it up, snapped the light off, and went to bed. Just as I fell asleep I prayed my first real prayer: *Please, God, help me get through tomorrow.*

I fell asleep before God could answer.

♌

In the morning I tried to work on algebra at the breakfast table, but it really wasn't happening. Of course we started the day with math. Mrs. Moffett was such a fanatic about homework that I figured I'd tell her before she could ask me. I stood by her desk and showed her what I'd done so far. "I'm sorry," I said. "I had rehearsal and then religion classes, and when I got home I was so tired."

"That's okay," Mrs. Moffett said. "You're going to be pretty busy today too, not to mention Friday. Why don't you finish it over the weekend?"

Well. Score one for God.

"I hear you're doing a great job in the play," she added. "We're all looking forward to seeing you."

At lunch Jenna showed me how she'd spent her evening. After rehearsal she'd gone through the script and figured out the cues for every single curtain. She'd written the set changes for every scene. She'd made copies of these lists for everybody.

Mrs. Sumner was delighted. She taped copies of Jenna's lists all over the place. In theory, we couldn't miss curtain cues now.

In practice, we still missed them all over the place. Yikes. Mrs. Sumner going ballistic on Wednesday was nothing compared to how ballistic she went on Thursday afternoon. I honestly thought she was going to start yanking parts right then, with one rehearsal left to go. We didn't have understudies. Backstage two girls fought over a lost tube of mascara. Chris's jaw stuck out and I could see how hard he was working to keep a lid on his temper. I mostly just felt tired.

We did the kitchen table scene. I looked at Chris and tried to see a beloved older brother going off to war. I tried to imagine him going away, and me—Ruthie—worrying that I'd never see him again. I thought of him dying.

It didn't help. I was looking at Chris, not Joe. I didn't think it was Chris's fault. I also wasn't sure it was mine.

"Do you think we're just not good enough?" I asked him, when Mrs. Sumner finally let us take a break and get some water from the drinking fountain in the hall.

He drummed his fingers against his legs, the way he did whenever he was nervous. "No," he said. "I think we're just not there yet. Gotta dig deep for this one." He stared off in the distance as he spoke. No one took drama more seriously than Chris.

"What does Ruthie want?" he asked me. "You're Ruthie. What do you want?"

I thought. In that one scene I wanted Joe not to leave, of course, but that wasn't the whole answer. I thought of the whole play, and of the book it was based on, which Mrs. Sumner had given me to read. "I want my family to see who I really am," I said slowly. I had thought all along that because Ruthie was so loud, everyone could see her; but now I realized it wasn't true. "I want them to listen to me. And I feel like Joe—you—are the only one who does. I'm afraid . . . afraid I'll lose that, along with you."

Chris's eyes widened. I grinned at him. He whispered, "Bingo."

"What do you want?" I asked. "As Joe."

"I want to stay home," he said, without hesitation. "Everything I want out of life is at home, but I can't have it. I can't stay home. Because of the war I've got to go away."

This was very sad. It was very real. I felt, when we started over from the top, that everything was going to be different now.

It wasn't. Chris and I were almost there, but not quite. I could put Ruthie on over myself, I could move the way she would and talk the way she would, and react the way she would, but I couldn't quite get rid of myself. Neither, I thought, could Chris. But we were close—closer than we'd been so far.

"Much better!" Mrs. Sumner said at the end, when we were all sitting on the stage. "Finally! That's the kind of rehearsal we need." She gave out several pages of notes, then told us to set up for the first scene, hang up our costumes, and put our props on the prop table. "Tomorrow after announcements we come straight here," she said. "First show at nine thirty."

I didn't expect her to say anything about my scene, and she didn't. I knew we were almost there.

I headed out to where my mom was waiting for me. I felt so much less tired now. I felt really fine.

Q

I went to sleep feeling happy and confident about the play. I woke up in the middle of the night with my throat closing in panic. What was my first line?

CHAPTER
29

I couldn't remember. I absolutely couldn't. I stared at the ceiling, and forced myself to breathe. I pictured the boys running onstage, me running after. "Give it back! Give it back!" That was my first line. Then what? For the life of me, I couldn't remember. I pictured myself onstage, tongue-tied, every word I'd ever memorized forgotten. In my mind I looked like I've been carved from wood.

I'd be horrible. I'd wreck the show. Everyone would laugh—except my parents, who would say it was no more than they expected.

I forced myself to breathe slowly and steadily. I knew my lines. I knew Ruthie. I got up and found my script, and read a few pages by the dim green light from the numbers on my clock radio. This was very hard to do, and it made me tired. Gratefully, I slid back toward sleep.

Why couldn't I believe Jesus was the Son of God? All of a sudden I wanted to, more than anything. I wanted to be baptized and forgiven and blessed. I wanted to hold the Eucharist and realize that it really was the body of Christ. I wanted all that.

I was wide awake again. I looked at my script. No answers

there. I thrashed around for a while, trying to make my pillow more comfortable, and then I took another deep breath and followed Mrs. Brashares's advice.

I talked to Jesus.

In the middle of the night, I emptied everything out of my mind except this one thing, this wanting to believe. I held on to that. And then I talked to someone I didn't believe existed, someone I didn't believe could answer.

"Jesus," I said, "I'd really like to believe."

Nothing happened. No lightning, no clap of thunder. I didn't get knocked out of my bed the way Paul got knocked off his horse on the way to Damascus. I waited. I quieted my mind, shooed away all the thoughts of Paul and Mrs. Brashares and horses and Damascus and Ruthie and my parents. I started to feel sleepy again.

Then I heard, quiet but clear like a tiny bell, an answer.
Okay.

Whenever we arrived at school too early we had to wait in the cafeteria until it was time to go to our rooms. The next morning, I got ready fast and hustled Mom to get me to school ahead of time, and she agreed because she thought I was wound up about the play. I was, of course.

Chris stood in front of the cafeteria door getting chewed out by the teacher on early duty. I waited until the teacher started yelling at someone else, then pulled him into the hallway. "Come with me," I said.

"She took away my baseball."

"You were throwing a baseball in the cafeteria?"

"Wasn't *throwing* it. Just sort of bouncing it."

We climbed the steps to the church. I went through the doors and found Father Micah in the sacristy, taking off the vestments he wore for early-morning Mass. A whole bunch of old people were standing around. "I talked to Jesus," I told Father Micah. "He said it was no problem that I didn't believe in him yet. He said to go ahead."

Chris's eyebrows shot up. "How can you—never mind." He laughed.

Father Micah just smiled. He finished hanging his chasuble

in the closet, and he went back to his office and came out carrying a big leather-covered book and a pen. He opened the book of the elect, and I carefully signed my name.

❧

I had not been transformed into a believer. I had been transformed into someone who was willing to believe. I knew the difference. I knew I'd get there eventually.

❧

At the theater everyone was nervous. Nobody cracked jokes today. The girls put on makeup—I had to borrow some from Jenna, because I forgot about it. We changed into our costumes. Mrs. Sumner came backstage to warn us to be quiet, because the first classes were already filing into their seats. She formed us into a circle, and, just like with the Christmas play, we prayed a quick Our Father.

I sat waiting on one of the set pieces in the wings. I was nervous, but it was a useful sort of nervousness and I didn't mind it. I considered testing out this Jesus stuff and praying that I remembered my lines, but I also thought that Jesus probably didn't care one way or another about my part in this play. Anyway, I thought I could remember my lines without help. All that remained was to get rid of myself completely—get rid of Abby, and put on Ruthie. I sat and I thought, and then I tried to not think. When I heard Mrs. Sumner start her curtain speech I stood up. Chris stood

171

beside me, and around us all the boys who played Ruthie's older brothers. From the wings across the stage, Jenna gave me a thumbs-up before she yanked the curtain open.

We were on.

We weren't perfect, but we were good. We were quite good, and some of us were very good. No one missed a line or a cue or a curtain. Not one curtain; a miracle.

We reached the scene where Joe leaves. Chris and I sat on chairs at the kitchen table. We were looking right at each other, though we had to turn out a little so the audience could see us. We talked back and forth. He wasn't Chris right now, he was Joe. I was Ruthie. I could feel all the sadness in the air between us. I could feel how much Ruthie loved Joe, and how much she depended on him, and I realized how alone she—I—was going to be when he was gone. I felt that if I took my eyes away from him he'd already be gone. Joe—Chris—whichever—stood up. He said his last lines with a sort of desperation that brought me to my feet as well, and I—Ruthie—whatever—threw my arms around him with a gulping sob. He put his arms around me, very gently, because I was one of the things he treasured most. We held perfectly still while the curtain closed. In the audience not a person made a sound.

CHAPTER
31

It wasn't written in the script like that. It was better our way. It was *right*. I was so pleased, I was almost shaky, but I had three scenes left. Chris didn't; he sat down backstage and watched from the wings.

At the end there was lots of applause, and then the curtain shut. We were supposed to stay quietly backstage until the theater emptied, but we weren't quiet at all. We screamed and laughed and jumped up and down, because we did well. I laughed, but I didn't scream. I was too happy to scream.

Mrs. Sumner came backstage, smiling and laughing and giving people high fives. I saw her say, "Good job, Chris." He looked at her anxiously, without smiling at all. I wanted to bop him. Didn't he know he was good?

Mrs. Sumner paused and wrinkled her brow. "Very well done," she said.

"Okay." He looked less sure of himself than I'd ever seen him.

"Aren't you happy?" I asked.

He shrugged. "It can always be better."

"I don't think so," I said.

It did get better, just a tiny bit. It flowed a little more

smoothly, and some people finally found their way into their roles. No one made any big mistakes. It was a glorious day, one of the most glorious of my life. At the end of the evening performance I couldn't quit smiling. I didn't even realize how hard I was smiling until my cheeks started to ache.

"Very good, Abby," my mom said quietly.

Of course I'd known they were watching—they drove me to the theater, after all—but I'd forgotten about them when I was onstage. Maybe Chris cared what other people thought about his acting. I didn't. What *I* thought was good enough.

CHAPTER

32

"I need a new dress for Easter," I said at breakfast Saturday morning.

My mom checked her watch. "Okay," she said. "I've got to go to the office for a few hours, but you can come with me. We'll go to the mall from there. Are there any rules? Do you need to wear white for your baptism?"

"White!" Dad looked alarmed. "You don't have to wear a veil, do you?"

"No," I said. "And it doesn't have to be white. I just want a nice spring dress."

"Huh." He snapped his newspaper and grumbled, "I suppose I'll have to wear a suit."

I looked up. "You don't have to come," I said.

"I was kidding," he said quickly. "I wouldn't miss it."

"Well, suits are optional," I said. "I don't care what you wear. I won't be sitting with you, anyway, I've got to sit with Mrs. Brashares up front."

"What time does it start?"

"I have to be there at seven," I said. "The Mass starts at eight. At midnight there's a big party in the school cafeteria."

Dad wrinkled his brow. "Is it important to you that we go back for that?" he asked.

There wouldn't be any *going back*. Mrs. Brashares had told me that the Vigil Mass would last between three and a half and four hours. I thought about telling my dad this. I decided not to. He was trying, after all.

☙

"Explain to me about forgiveness," I asked Mrs. Brashares. We were on our way to the rehearsal for the Easter service, so we could learn where to stand in line for our baptisms and stuff like that.

"What do you need explained?" We were almost to the church parking lot, and when she pulled in, she parked and looked at me patiently.

"Well . . . what if I don't feel like forgiving someone? What if I'm pretty sure that person doesn't want me to forgive them, doesn't think they even need to be forgiven?"

She tilted her head. "Who are we talking about here?"

"That boy—"

"Ah. You don't think he's sorry?"

I shook my head. "He enjoyed being nasty. He liked it. He's not sorry."

"And you think, for you to forgive him, he needs to be sorry?"

"It would be nice," I said. "I mean, we're supposed to be sorry, aren't we? We're supposed to ask for forgiveness?"

The creases in her forehead smoothed out while she thought. "I love your questions, Abby, I do. We *are* supposed to be sorry. And what that boy did was wrong, flat-out wrong."

"Chris told you?"

She nodded. "But, if you don't forgive him, it changes you, not him. And if you do forgive him, it changes you, not him. Forgiving someone is about you, not about the other person."

I sighed. This was another day when I felt like backing out. "I don't feel like forgiving him," I said. "I like being angry." It gave me energy. It gave me power.

"Sure," she said. "Sometimes I like being angry too. But in the long run, forgiveness feels better."

CHAPTER
33

We sat in the pew, waiting. The light from the parking lot shone bright on the lilies around the altar. It was Easter Vigil, but still, nothing was happening. I fumbled with the candle in my hands. I shifted my weight impatiently.

From the back of the church I heard a sudden scritch, like a match striking, and suddenly the whole back end of the church was alight. Flames shot up, higher, higher. I craned my neck to see, and Chris put his hand on my shoulder and stood on his toes. There was a cauldron of some sort, gleaming copper on a pedestal, and the cauldron was full of fire. Father Micah stood beside it, his arms held high. I hoped his vestments wouldn't catch fire. Incense filled the air with choky perfume.

The fire was beautiful. I couldn't take my eyes from it.

Someone brought out a huge white candle, and Father Micah lit it with a taper he stuck into the bonfire. He chanted in Latin; the churchful of people responded.

Lumen Christi. The Light of Christ.

Deo Gratias. Thanks be to God.

I'd never heard the words before, but they were easy to pick up, and before the congregation had repeated them twice I joined in. Chris sang at my shoulder. His voice was clear and pitch-perfect; he soared.

I wondered if my parents were singing. I wondered what they thought of the wild bonfire, the chanting. It felt to me like a ritual from the start of time, like something Abraham would have done.

Lumen Christi. Deo Gratias.

The music started to crack me open. I could feel it, feel myself begin to tremble. Religion wasn't a game, I knew that now. It was fire, right in the church, and lightning might in fact strike me down.

Father Micah lifted the huge candle high. *"Lumen Christi,"* he sang. "Light of Christ."

"Deo Gratias. Thanks be to God."

He processed slowly up the aisle. I waited on tiptoe. I was eager for the candle to reach the front. But halfway up the aisle Father Micah stopped, and slowly lowered the candle to head height. Someone came forward and lifted a taper to light it from the candle. Another person, and another.

I nudged Chris. "How come we don't get to do that?" The candle in my hands, the one the usher gave me, was much smaller than the tapers.

"Watch," said Chris.

The people with the tapers moved quickly up the aisles. They went from pew to pew, and the people standing at the ends of the pews lit their skinny candles from the tapers. The people beside them lit their candles from the first people's.

As I watched, light spread through the church. Someone lit Chris's candle. He lit mine, and I lit Mrs. Brashares's. I looked down at the tiny flickering flame.

The whole church glowed from candlelight. Shadows danced, flames flickered. Father Micah carried the Easter candle up to the altar and fixed it in a holder there. Light shone everywhere.

People read Scripture by the light of the candles. Seven readings—a compromise, Father Micah had told me, between the eleven you were allowed to do and the five that were considered the minimum. "Pay attention when they're read all together," he said. "They tell the story of our salvation."

I'd have liked to have listened, but there was so much else going on: Father Micah's glittering vestments, the candles and flowers everywhere, the chants and the flames and the thick, pungent incense. "Smells and bells," Chris murmured. It was amazing to me how holy it felt.

And yet. I knew I didn't really believe. All I had was that one whispered word, in the middle of the night. It might have been a hallucination. It was probably a dream.

The lights came up in the church for the reading of the Gospel, and afterwards we blew our little candles out. I was sorry; the ordinary light seemed too thin and bright after those warm little flames. Father Micah preached a homily. I knew I should listen, but the words sounded like static over the radio, because of what was coming next. I shouldn't have been afraid—last week was the hard part—but I was.

The sermon ended. Everyone in the church stirred restlessly. Father Micah stood, and asked the elect to come forward.

That meant us non-baptized. There were nineteen of us, all the way from old Mr. Spanish to a pair of two-year-old twins whose mom and dad were getting baptized too. Mrs. Hall called our names to come forward.

"Abigail Catherine Lorenzo, come to the waters of Baptism."

Mrs. Brashares and I stood.

The group of the elect and their sponsors looked hilarious. The sponsors were dressed way up—Mrs. Brashares actually wore makeup—and the elect had on shorts and T-shirts, and flip-flop sandals. I was wrong about dipping my hands into the baptismal font. There was another font, like a bathtub, sunk into the floor behind the raised one. We were going to get wet.

When Mrs. Hall called Mr. Spanish's name, the whole church went still. His sponsor had to help him stand, and Mr. Spanish's legs trembled as he pushed his walker forward. He wore horrible faded bathing trunks, and his legs were purple and black.

We'd been so worried about him the last few weeks. He was pretty much just waiting to die. Father Micah had offered to baptize him weeks ago, and give him Holy Communion, and everything, but he insisted he wanted to stay with the rest of us. Every Catholic class ended with us all praying, hard, that he'd make it. Now he stood in front of the altar with tears pouring down his face, and his sponsor's face, and pretty nearly everyone's faces. Even mine.

We processed to the back of the church while a cantor led the congregation in the Litany of Saints. I'd heard it sung once before, on All Saints' Day, the day after Halloween. "St. John the Baptist," the cantor intoned, and the congregation sang, "Pray for us."

"St. Peter and St. Paul . . ."

"Pray for us."

"St. Mary Magdalene . . ."

"Pray for us."

I was nearly to the back when I had a sudden feeling of panic. I whipped my head around. I was looking for my mother.

I found her. She'd moved from her seat out to the aisle, where she could see the baptismal font. She held a camera. When she saw me looking at her, she waved and smiled.

Was it going to be okay, then? Would everything be okay?

We stood in line in front of the Jacuzzi baptismal font. A big pink shell sat on one edge of it, and a tall stack of white towels. Father Micah blessed the water. Somehow this involved sticking part of the Easter candle into it. It took forever. I shivered.

Next came the Baptismal Promises.

Do you reject Satan?

I do. (No problem on that one.)

And all his works?

I do.

And all his empty promises?

I do.

Do you believe in God, the Father Almighty, creator of heaven and Earth?

I do.

Do you believe in Jesus Christ, his only Son, our Lord, who was born of the Virgin Mary, was crucified, died, and was buried, rose from the dead, and is now seated at the right hand of the Father?

I took a deep breath.

I do. (I'd do my best.)

Mrs. Brashares's hand closed very gently on my shoulder.

Do you believe in the Holy Spirit, the holy catholic church, the communion of saints, the forgiveness of sins, the resurrection of the body, and life everlasting?

The only one there I really still struggled with was the forgiveness of sins. But I said,

I do.

Father Micah beamed at us. He said, "God the all-powerful Father of our Lord Jesus Christ has given us new birth by water and the Holy Spirit, and forgiven all our sins. May he also keep us faithful to our Lord Jesus Christ for ever and ever. Amen."

And then the baptisms began. I was close to the front, but Mr. Spanish was first. His sponsor and three or four other men picked him right off the ground and carefully lowered him into the font. Father Micah scooped water into the big shell, poured water over Mr. Spanish's head, and shouted, "I baptize you in the name of the Father, and of the Son, and of the Holy Spirit."

Mr. Spanish didn't cry. He lifted his face while the water ran down it, and his eyes looked as wondrous as a little child's. Then the men hoisted him. They helped him towel off, and go out through the door.

A woman went next, then a teenaged boy, then another woman. Then it was my turn. I stepped carefully into the water. It was warm, like a nice bath. I looked up. Standing just behind Father Micah, right in my line of vision, were my parents, and Chris. Mom took a photo as the first wave of water went over my head.

I baptize you in the name of the Father, and of the Son, and of the Holy Spirit.

I felt it.

I was forgiven.

Everything I'd done wrong washed away into the water. All the anger that led me to take a knife to school. All the guilt from what happened next. All my fury at my parents, for not paying attention to what was happening.

My sins were gone. Right now, for this one moment, my soul was perfectly clean. It was my own personal miracle. I dropped my head, and thought the words *thank you*. Then I realized I was praying.

I'd leaped. I believed.

✎

I didn't know you could *choose* to believe in salvation. I didn't know it could be that easy. "You have put on Christ," Father Micah said later in the Mass, after we elect had changed into good clothes and towel-dried and combed our sopping wet hair. We'd put on Christ the way I'd put on Ruthie, except that I wouldn't be taking Christ off.

The Vigil Mass lasted two more hours. I lit my own baptismal candle and was anointed and confirmed, and took Communion, but all the while a part of my mind thought about my baptism. I wondered if the photographs would show what really happened. I didn't imagine they could.

"Wow," Dad said, when I caught up with them just outside the church doors. "That was a lot of church."

Mom said, "You looked nice, Abigail. You looked . . . happy."

All around us, people swirled down the stairs to the party, talking and laughing. Everyone seemed connected, except my parents. I knew they were trying, but they weren't quite there. *Forgiveness works both ways,* I thought. *Eventually, I'll forgive them too.*

It would be hard, but not impossible.

Chris barreled up the stairs. "Hey, Abby! They've got shrimp! Hurry up!"

"What about chocolate?" I shouted back. "I gave up chocolate for Lent, remember?"

He stopped at the top of the stairs and knocked the hair out of his eyes. "Tons of chocolate," he said. "Hurry *up.*"

ℓℓℓℓℓℓ